THE TALES OF
BUL BUL ADVENTURES

THE TALES OF
BUL BUL ADVENTURES

JAWAD AL BAHRANI

PARTRIDGE
A Penguin Random House Company

To order additional copies of this book, contact
Toll Free 800 101 2657 (Singapore)
Toll Free 1 800 81 7340 (Malaysia)
orders.singapore@partridgepublishing.com

www.partridgepublishing.com/singapore

CONTENTS

PREFACE

In the course of lifetime, one passes through many channels in the attempt to fine his destiny. Each of these channels becomes a test of his integrity as he tries to decide the one that is best suited for his ambitions. Like many before us, who have spent a lifetime in search of a solution to their problems, by a way of learning and preserving the knowledge they acquired. Scientists, writers, historians and others, have dedicated their lives, for the better and never for the worst, smoothing out delicate matters for the sake of learning

To me, writing is not only a hobby but is a channel of life where I can find recognition through my readers. I write things that come into my mind such as poetry, personal thoughts and quotations. Story writing is a new experience to me and this is the first one. I began writing this book in the early 60s and yet for some reason, it has never been to a publisher or any other public institution. It has remained with me for more than fifty years, and now at the age of seventy nine, I hope to live long enough to see it published and read by many.

My imagination might have changed a little since than but I am still as religious as I ever was and my faith in Islam is still as strong as it was then. My story is more fiction than fact. Its setting is based on fictitious events that happened over two hundred years ago. I let my imagination run free to try to exploit in full the spiritual power which I feel even two centuries ago was no the age such witchcraft and sorcery could still be practiced. But as a devout Muslim, I know that only God can empower a human being into performing such supernatural trickery. In my story, I can be accused of being too excessive in my exploitation of the supernatural and if you, dear reader, feel that way, then I accept the criticism in good faith. All I ask from you, in return, is to be fair in your judgement, that I am not the only one to do so.

In this light, then I should ask you to extend your criticism to the producers of the X-Files TV series, the film makers of Exorcism, The Aliens and Odyssey, among many who entertained millions in their absurdity. I believe that they all have to same intentions as mine and that is to add spice in their stores by making them more interesting to read or view. I just wrote this story with the same enthusiasm as the original writers of Sindbad, Ali Baba and Aladdin, not expecting you to believe in the impossible but merely to entertain you.

So I ask my readers to believe what they can accept and reject what they cannot. It is not my intentions to insult the intelligence of my readers but to entertain and give pleasure. I myself admit that no human being alive today possess such powers and the ages of miracles and over. Such things did indeed exist in the past, in the way of God, who granted special powers to various individuals in different ages, to do good, thought abused at times.

Let our children continue to enjoy stories like "One Thousand And One Night" and the likes of my book which I present to them. Our children can learn, in their imagination, that what could happen centuries ago, cannot possible happen in this day and age. In letting their imaginations run free, they can lose themselves, at least for an hour or so, in the world of fantasy.

It is well known that whenever there is a history, there is an event and whenever there is a story, then there is a teller behind it. The teller is always inspired by his own thoughts and it is up to the reader to believe or not. Lastly, I would like to stress out that although the setting of this story is based on a few countres, it should not reflect in any way to their culture, people or history. It is purely based on fiction and its events or characters have no resemblance to places or people who are either alive or dead. I ask the authority concern of the countries I mention in my story to bare with me with the good side intention of my thoughts and never the ill side intentions did I have within me. God be my witness.

The author,
Jawad Ibrahim Ahmed

ACKNOWLEDGMENT

Somewhere far away, in the East African coast of the Indian Ocean, where its sea waves fade away with a cool morning breeze on the white sands of the most inhabitant beaches, as clean as flour, as soft as powder. No, you will not believe my words until you have to be there yourself, the jewels of Africa, the islands of spices, the cosmopolitan of man civilizations.

It was on the 28th of October 1935, on one of these two islands, in the island of Zanzibar, at a place known as Stone town in mkunazini, I was born by two wonderful parents, very kind people who share all their love to us, who have immigrated from Oman and chose Zanzibar as their second home, and for that I am so grateful for their decision, and all because I grew up in a place where Islam is the No.1 religion, then follows the Christianity and then Hinduism. I grew up in a country where neighbours care and love their neighbours, where one experience no discrimination of any, colour, race or religion, just like the way it is in Oman, tolerance is the way of our living.

All my Islamic and school education I learned there, where I gain my English language as well as general knowledge, thanks to my parents who believe that schools were necessary for us. Thought my standard of education was not as high as my dreams were, I just finished secondary school with the help of self taught by my friends, but I learned, and now I am able to write things and express myself well and be understood with my poor English.

My parents were simple people, religious minded, who believed in preserving their (Gems) children by enforcing strict rules. My father was a man of principle, he believed that, no under age kids should be allowed to be outside home after six o'clock in the evening, that Qur'an teaching and learning is compulsory, so whether we liked it or not, we had to obey him, and frankly I did not like it at that time, thought it was meant for our own good but could never realise why. But as we grew up to become men with our own responsibilities, our own families and bare our own children (Gems), then we understood why.

Zanzibar is a very beautiful place to live. Quite and friendliness, peaceful and helping hands are yours just for asking. Your neighbour's children are as yours as well your's to them. What one cook, can share it with her neighbour and she will receive from her, her cooking so to get variety of dishes in todays menu. When one neighbour who is so close to her, going for shopping, whatever she will buy for herself will buy for her friend neighbour as well, maybe a pair of Khanga (two pieces of cloth material well decorated with four sides design border, so clourful, traditionally many East African women wear them, also in Yemen and Oman are common), she may buy a pair for her neighbour, while in return that good neighbour maybe will also return something to show her appreciation on the given gift, will cook a very popular egg bread known as "Mkate wa mayai" of which Zanzibaries cook only on special occasions. So these are attitudes or your may call the way of life for the Zanzibari people.

They are always toghether in many events and occasions, such as weddings, funerals, visiting the sick people in hospitals as well as attending daily prayers either in Mosques or Churches. Even in neighbourhood if there is aquerral, everybody would be concerned to try to solve or come to understanding of the two querraling people by using words of wisdom in making them realise that querraling worth nothing more than torments and misunderstandings.

For me, although for now I am living far away from these nice people of whom I am so much attached to, lived and grew with them since my birth, people of whom I have mixed my blood with, people of who I can speak their language so well as same as my parents tongue, yet I can not forget these people for many reasons or other, neither forget Zanzibar, my birth place, the soil of were I bury my umblical cord (to Zanzibaris, this means that that land is part of you and is where you belong).

I may call myself a person with two destinies, Why? Because I love so much the past of where I was and do the same to where I am now, my origin. Though till this day, where all my parents were born and live here in Oman, yet I am, and as well some other Zanzibar Omanis who were like me once lived in Africa or Asia are known and refer to as Zanzibaris, etc., I personally do not mind at all because it is fact that I am an Omani born in Zanzibar, and frankly am proud and happy and feel honoured with dignity that I am a person with two destinies.

When I started to write this story of "THE ADVANTURES OF BUL BUL" in 1964, all my imaginations were that Bul Bul was a figure from Zanzibar and and among the the people of Zanzibar because I had and still have these feelings that Zanzibar needs more regocnition (though political and economical situation were not steady) but Zanzibar needs any helping and deserve to let the world know it more than just reading a word ZANZIBAR from any printing material. Here I would like to point clean, I am not a politician never did I was one and will never like to be in that platform of those who for one reason or another created Zanzibar in a very bad impression till today one do not know whom to trust and whom to ingore. Here I am speaking for my people of Zanzibar since my childhood, for their goodness, their cultures, their way of life and so on. I pray to God that "oh! Allah, prise Zanzibar and its people for their best and not for their worst, make them be as they used to be, please bless them with all your blessings." I hope that after reading my book many out of many of this world beings, will pay a visit to these jewels of Africa, this land of my Bul Bul, and their visit may create a history of not to forget, that visit to the islands of spices will be for the best and never the worst.

I am taking this opportunity to express my thanks to each and all who have helped me and gave their helping hand as well in accomplishing my dreams in becoming a story writer. So many individuals who in one way or the other, share their value time, in either listening or reading or typing of this story of my childish imaginations, yet I believe that this book is worth reading and should be red by many.

In thanking so many individuals for their rendering on service for me or another, there is one particular person whom I can never be able to repay his pain taking service for me, he is His Excelency Mr. Ahmed Humoud Al Ma'mary, the former Oman ambassador to India, who with out hesition accepted my request of translating this story from swahili into English, there is no words what-so-ever either sweet or wise will be equal to repay his gratitudes for me. As he is no longer with us now, passed away about three to four years now, I raise my hands to God for prayers and ask him to rest his soul in heaven, amin. Lastly I would like to thank my nephew, Mr Saleh Abbas al Shaibani for English grammar correction, he did his best, Thank you Saleh. As well as not forgeting two of my grandchildren, Mr. Humud Al Sumri and Mr. Nadhim Al bahrani for their helping hand in making computer graphic work of the front and back cover of my book, while all design were part of my imagination creation. Thank you so much Humud and Nadhim, my helping hands. Last yesr 2013, I travel to Zanzibar looking for the right person to do the ilistrations for my book, searching in many corners of Zanzibar stone, I found a shop sailing paintings, the art paitnings which were hanging on the wall of that shop, drew my attention and made me to enter and inqure who was the painter of those piecies of art, the shopkeeper introduce to painter by telephone converzation, I made a deal with to do thye illustration work for me, we agree and he took all the initiative to make the illustration in my book, I will not forget Mr Ali Misifa of Zanzibar Tanzania for his illustration work he did for me under my instruction, he did the right job to my satisfaction. Also among all whom I have to thank is my wife Saida, who bare with me all the time of writing even in the middle of midnight, Thank you Saida and othe members of my family whom they share their thoughts, or give me ideas one way or another.

Thank you all your good people and God bless you.
The author.
Jawad Ibrahim Ahmed Al Bahrani

THE ADVENTURES OF BUL BUL

by

Jawad Ibrahim Ahmed Al Bahrani

During the last two centuries, there lived in the island of Zanzibar an old man called Mustafa the tailor. He was a very popular man in the islands and was well known in the whole of East Africa for his good and clean work of tailoring and embroidering man's gowns and loinclothes as well as caps.

Such types of dress were favourite to the people of the islands and those who lived along the coastline of East Africa.

The customers used to buy from Mustafa the gowns and handmade caps in advance of their being tailored that before they were completely tailored. They were ready to pay any price for such commodities. People of the islands of Zanzibar were not happy to wear gowns or caps, which were not tailored by Mustafa the tailor. A person feels proud to wear a cloth, which has been tailored by Mustafa. Also a gown or a cap tailored by Mustafa would be considered a precious gift to friends. Thus, Mustafa the tailor established a reputation for his good work and that is why he was known as Mustafa the tailor. However, his popularity ceased after his death.

Mustafa left a Son who was called Bul Bul who was fourteen years old when his father died. Bul Bul did not bother to learn the skill and trade of his father although his father Mustafa made every effort to train his son in this trade but in vein. Bul Bul wasted his time in useless games, which were useful neither to himself nor to his parents. He was more concerned in catching birds, picking up the unwanted fish in the beaches and such types of activities which lazy children prefer to do. Thus, being deceived by his youthfulness, Bul Bul could not realize that there is an end for every being, and that a day would come when his father would cease to exist and everything would be on his shoulders. He never thought about these facts and he simply continued to please himself with his useless hobbies. Such types of enjoyments are exactly as the saying goes "the enjoyment of a dog sitting on its tail".

After his father's death, Bul Bul continued with his day to day activities, and in most cases he would return home late and ask his mother to cook food for him, when he brought nothing with him. Unfortunately Mustafa did not leave any property when he died, and hence the life of Bul Bul and his mother was miserable. Bul Bul remembered the old days when his father was alive and the happy life they had. He then realized that what he had been doing was futile as there was nothing to eradicate the poverty he was experiencing. He decided to do something which would help him to earn a living and to help his mother.

After some time when Bul Bul was tired of roaming and as he took rest on the way, thoughts of the difficulties he was suffering came to his mind, remembering the useless activities which had occupied his mind when his father was alive.

His friends appeared and found him deep in thoughts recalling his old days. They told him to join them in their futile activities. He replied to them saying: "Oh my friends, I have been here for quite a long time and I was engaged in thoughts which concern all of us.

These activities which we have been practicing since our childhood are useless to us. Who amongst you can tell me what advantage we can derive from these activities which can help us and our parents? Just consider those pigeons which we used to kill and deprive them of their lives; what benefit have derived from our cruelty, or those birds we used to catch and even kill some of them! What did we get out of that? Also such remains of small fish we used to pick up from the fishermen! Whose belly among ours was filled up with it? Please answer me my friends! What difference is there between us and the vagabonds? We have wasted all our youthfulness in the useless activities. We have been thrown out from the Qur'aan teaching schools and the secular schools because of our engagement in these activities. Let us ask ourselves the benefit we have derived by running away from the schools! Our friends who behaved well and worked hard in their studies some of whom have successfully completed their studies and have become teachers and clerks – were they ignorant to remain at school; If they were ignorant – supposedly – are we wise? Please answer me my friends!

Bul Bul's friends remained quiet and listened to him. Many of them consented that Bul Bul has spoken the truth as they have done nothing which they themselves appreciate and which has pleased their parents. When Bul Bul drew his friends into his thought provoking ideas, he himself was contemplating quietly that if only he had realised earlier and listened to his father and abandoned those useless activities he would have been quiet a different person altogether.

After a long silence, one of his friends said after listening to his words: "I will answer you! I believe there is a better and easier way to help us get rid of our problems!! One of their friends was anxious to know what was the idea, and their friends continued and said: "The best way which I see can help us is to go and steal". When Bul Bul heard such a stupid proposal shouted: "That is your own havoc! I am not with you". Another friend opposed Bul Bul and said: "Friends! Do you not see the Bul Bul begins to leave us? If it is true that our activities are bad, why has he been with us all this time? Why was he joining us?". Bul Bul said: "Look my friends! Every time a human being grows old, his mind also grows up. Who amongst you has realized earlier that our way of life and the activities we are engaged in are not useful for us? Who would like to be called a vagabond and people hate to see him every where he goes? Do you wish to remain in this way all our lives without trying to change our habits and character? My friends! we have to realize that we are now young men and sane and we have to abandon these useless activities. Time has come when we should give up these nonsensical things and seek means to earn rightful life which will help both ourselves and our parents".

Another friend who opposed Bul Bul stood up and said: "We have decided to do what we have said in order to please ourselves and we feel that your advise is contrary to our aspirations. If you have decided to change your habit, that is your own opinion. When we go home we have no problems; we are given clothes and we are given pocket money. So what difficulties do we suffer?"

Bul Bul then said: "My friend! You do not know what poverty means! Neither do you know what are the difficulties of poverty, and it seems that you do not know what it means to be without anything and what it means to seek something. Your life is plain – sailing, and hence I am not surprised to see you insisting upon maintaining this bad habit. I only advise those poor young men who experience problems of poverty in their lives similar to those which have affected me. If you, my colleagues, see that maintaining this kind of life is a good thing, then go ahead; but as for me, I am not with you, and from this moment, I am not one of you".

That group which Bul Bul was a member since childhood failed to understand his decision to leave them although among them there were some who supported his ideas. Those few who supported him were overpowered by the stubborn ones among whom one told Bul Bul: "Although you are now a young man, I believe that you are still a baby sucking milk at home because your statements are childish. I agree with you that this group does not suit you any longer because this is not the group of babies who still suck milk. So you had better go home to your mother to suck milk".

This statement annoyed Bul Bul and angered him very much but notwithstanding that, he could not do anything at that time because the group was big. He knew that if he attempted to fight that young man who told him that nonsense, he would have to fight the whole group. He thus left and just a few steps ahead, he picked up a stone and threw it at that youth who insulted him. Unfortunately, the stone hit an oldman who was passing by on his head. The old man touched the place which was hit and lamented. He went to Bul Bul and told him: "My son! Were it really you who hit me with the stone?" Bul Bul felt very bad and was puzzled, but finally consented and said: "Yes! It was I who hit you and please sir, pardon me! It was not intentionally. I meant to one of those boys, but unluckily it hit you!". The old man said: "I am not as strong as you are, able to throw a stone like this to passer by, but it does not matter". The old man took a coin from his pocket and gave it to Bul Bul saying: "Accept this gift for the good work you have done, and it is better if you continue with this habit because you may get much more gifts".

The old man left and Bul Bul was surprised how the old man responded. "How can an old man like this give me money after my hitting him with a stone? And giving me an advise that I should continue with hitting people with stone?

Bul Bul's friends were watching, and when the old man had gone, they approached him and asked him: "What did that old man give you?" He replied to them that after hitting the old man with a stone he gave him money and advised him to continue with the habit of hitting people with stones because it is a good habit and perhaps he may get better gifts. His friends were moved by the explanation which Bul Bul made and they decided to practice it themselves in the hope that they also may get better gifts.

A few minutes later another old man appeared wearing a cloak and a turban and had beard mixed white and black. He was not as weak as the first one, but appeared energetic and was carrying a load on his back. He seemed to be a stranger. Bul Bul's friends began to ask each other who would start hitting him. The young man who insulted Bul Bul decided to throw at the man and immediately threw a big stone at him. Painfully the old man held his forehead and went towards the young men. He asked them who threw a stone at him. The young man who threw the stone hurriedly replied to him: "I threw the stone! Give me my reward!". The old man told him that he was ready to pay him his reward. He kept his load down and gave him a very big blow, throwing him to the ground. Seeing that things became serious, Bul Bul's friends ran away, but Bul Bul in a puzzlement remained there. The old man went to him and told him: "If you and your friends have not been taught manners in your homes, I will teach you. He slapped Bul Bul heavily and told him to take him to his home where he can meet his people. He told him that he wanted to meet his people because it is they who did not teach him manners. When they reached Bul Bul's home, he knocked the door and Bul Bul's mother opened it. When she saw her son being held by an old man, she shouted: Oh my son, what calamity have you brought home today. Do you not stop your naughtiness?

The old man interrupted and told Bul Bul "Reply! Reply to your mother!". Bul Bul related the whole incident from the first time when he hit another old man with a stone and got a reward of money, to this old man who slapped him. His mother told him: "My son, are you so stupid to that extent? Where have you seen a person giving a reward for being hit with a stone? That was merely teaching you a lesson! Do you not understand yet?" She scolded him very much and told him that he deserved the punishment which received.

She told him that if he listened the teachings of his father nothing bad would have happened to him. "You were more concerned with your activities, and I see that it is better that this person should punish you more and more". She left him outside the house and went inside. Seeing his mother furious and angry, Bul Bul began to cry and ran after her into the house. He repeatedly said: "Mother! I have repented! I have repented! And I shall never repeat this folly again!". His mother said: "No! you have not repented yet and your mind is not yet matured; you are useless in this house. In spite of the difficulties which we have, you still make problems, and we always get complaints from the people". What is wrong with you – Oh my lord, what mercy have you granted me by giving me this child who is useless in this home!". Bul Bul cried more and begged his mother to accept his repentance and promised never to repeat his mistakes. He said: "I prefer to be slapped by you than being slapped by this old man again as I cannot bear his blow".

The old man who was all the time listening outside began to be sympathetic and he asked for permission to enter the house. He thought that if there was a way to help them he would certainly do so. When he entered the house he told Bul Bul's mother: "Excuse me Madam! I have realised from your words when you are scolding your son that it seems like the boy's father is not around. Can you tell me if this boy's father has traveled abroad? Or has he gone to work?". The lady replied: "My husband is dead, and that is why I get all these problems of looking after this boy". The old man said: "I feel that your son has now realised his mistakes after hearing your statements, and he may stop his bad activities and will adopt good manners as he promised. I believe that the punishment which he has received is sufficient to teach him the affairs of the world". Bul Bul was listening attentively the statement of the old man. The old man then turned to Bul Bul and asked him: "What is your name Oh young man?" Bul Bul replied: "My name is Bul Bul bin Mustafa and my father was popularly known as Mustafa the tailor." The old man told Bul Bul: "My son! A person is taught many things by the universe and also he is taught by the mistakes, which he makes. According to my understanding, I see that you have good understanding and according to your age, you are no longer a child but a smart young man. I do not think that you will repeat the mistakes you have been making." Bul Bul thanked the old man and said: "It is true that I have wasted my time in useless activities which have led me to come in contact with you in an unordinary way. It was at that particular time while sitting I have been thinking about these activities which have made me to be a young man who is useless and helpless to my mother, who needs my help. I consent that my mistakes are many and serious. I sincerely beg your pardon for all that has happened and I also seek my mother's forgiveness. I promise that I shall seek means by which I can help myself and my mother."

The old man said: "My son! Any parent, particularly, if he has a grown up child like you, will certainly forgive and be sympathetic after hearing a statement like yours." "I believe that you are now renowned and you will never again indulge yourself in vagabond activities. It is the prayers of the parents and their satisfaction, which make a person lead a happy and satisfactory life. Bul Bul, my son! Never abandon your mother. You should be with her and help her in everything she needs. Try to make her happy and to forget the shock which has come because of your fathers death." Bul Bul's mother sighed and said: "Who wants to see her son go astray and become abandoned? Who is happy to be in difficulties? "Luck sometimes plays with human beings, and that is test which requires patience, and success in such a test means success in life and failure therein means problems of life. I thank God for granting me patience, which has enabled me to pass this test and to be saved from the problems of this world which is full of evils. "My son, Bul Bul, if truly you have determined to abandon your childish activities and to become a wise young man and to seek means by which you can earn a living which will enable us to live like others, then my sincere blessings and forgiveness are with you." Bul Bul replied: "I promise, mother, that, that is what I shall do."

The old man being a stranger and being his first day to come to this island, told Bul Bul's mother: "My daughter! I am an old man who possesses no property, except my healing work by which I earn my living. This, your land is good and it appeals to the eyes and it is that which attracted me to come here, following the good reputation which are widely known throughout the world". "My name is Hashim and I was born in South Africa. I come from there where the roots of my ancestors are found. I left my country to seek knowledge of curing people in India and I have been there for fourty years. I have spent all my life to learn this knowledge and today I am one of the leading experts in this field. Give me Bul Bul so that I can teach him this knowledge in order that he may become a good healer to cure people and to gain a good reputation from the people. "I am ready to spend the rest of my life in these islands, which are well known." Bul Bul's mother did not know what to say at the beginning, as it was rather hard to agree immediately. On the other hand, however, she thought how Bul Bul was involved in bad activities, and thus she found it better for Bul Bul to be anything - even a spiritual healer, rather than being as he was. She then replied and said: "Surely your sympathy is great my elder but the decision is with Bul Bul himself, because it is he that you need. If he has no objection, then I have also agreed." Without hesitation Bul Bul said: "Mother! I accept the suggestion because hard work is better than a play, which is useless. Bul Bul's mother, seeing that the old man - Hakeem Hashim - was a stranger, she requested him to remain with them in the house and be their guest. Hakeem Hashim thanked them for their generosity and agreed to live with them as a member of the family.

BUL BUL IS
TAUGHT SCIENCE OF HEALING

H akeem Hashim began to teach Bul Bul the science of healing which he acquired after studying it for quite a long time. He taught him much regarding this knowledge such as ability to diagnose the patient through questioning and checking different parts of the body and to know the right medicine for the patient. He explained to Bul Bul everything about the human body and how the muscles work. He also taught him different kinds of illnesses, which affect people and how to cure them. He also taught him the incurable diseases and those, which lead to death. It took him many days until Bul Bul learnt enough to enable him to assure responsibility to heal patients. Hakeem Hashim himself continued to heal patients to earn his living. He became very popular in the islands. Hakeem Hashim knew other things besides his knowledge of healing but he never used this knowledge of such super natural power except when necessarily needed. He knew how to detect people who practiced witchcraft and the evil ones. He knew how to detect the thoughts of people without such people telling him their secrets. He also knew the science of hypnotism and could even instruct things to obey his orders but he never applied these things except when it became essential. He did not agree with those soothsayers who pretended to tell the fortune but tell lies which has no basis. Those practicing witchcraft were his enemies and because they feared him many of them began to disappear. He never agreed with anything, which contradicted with his religion of Islam in accordance with God's prohibition in his Qur'aan. He used to apply his knowledge to help people and to heal them, contrary to those who claimed to be healing whose work was to rob people of their money or to harm others for a trifle gain. These were the qualities and the knowledge, which Hakeem Hashim possessed.

One day Hakeem Hashim wanted to test his student to know if he had grasped the knowledge or not. One patient came to him and he decided to let Bul Bul deal with him. He told him: "Bul Bul, I want you to show me your expertise today so that I know if you have learnt the work I have been teaching you for quite a long time now. This patient is yours and I shall just be watching. You have to heal him."

Bul Bul did not hesitate at all but was not free from fear of not having learnt the job properly. He began to deal with his (first) patient.

The patient was suffering from weakness and became lean without knowing what exactly affected him. He never felt any pain in any part of his body. He just found that his weight was decreasing and was becoming weak. It was a big test for Bul Bul to diagnose a patient who did not know himself what was affecting him. Bul Bul began to examine his patient to find out what was affecting him. He examined every part of his body – the colour of his eyes, his tongue, his pulse and his heart beatings. All his efforts were useless, as he could not detect any sign of illness. Hakeem Hashim was watching Bul Bul while he was examining the patient.

Suddenly Bul Bul recalled in his mind that if the patient has no sign of a disease, which caused his weakness and leanness, then there must be something which worries him. He told his teacher Hakeem Hashim: "I want you to hypnotise this patient". Hakeem Hashim did not object and he hypnotised the patient. He used the method of telling the patient: "You feel sleepy!!! You need to sleep!!! Sleep!!! Sleep!" The patient began to become sleepy and drowsy and slowly began to close his eyes and finally he fell asleep.

Bul Bul told Hakeem Hashim: "There must be something which makes him week without being sick. The easy way to understand his problem is to ask the patient himself without his knowledge that he is being asked. That is why I asked you to hypnotize him so that we can ask him questions; perhaps we may get to know his problem." Bul Bul began to talk to the patient in his state of drowsiness and said: "Do you hear me?" The patient did not reply. He went closer to him and spoke to him in a very polite voice; "How about now! Do you hear me?" The patient began to nod very politely and said; "Yes! I hear you". Bul Bul continued; "Tell me! Who am I?" And he replied; "I do not know you". Bul Bul said; "there are questions I want to ask you and I would like you to answer me". The patient said; "Yes! Ask me!" Bul Bul asked him: What is worrying you? The patient repeated the word worrying... worrying.... Which worry? "Bul Bul told him: "I am a friend - a sincere friend who wants to help you, but I will not be able to help you until you tell me what is worrying you; perhaps I can help you and get you out of your problem. Now tell me if there is something, which is worrying you, or perhaps you have suspicious on a certain matter or perhaps you like something or somebody and it is difficult to realise your wish. "Please tell me what is your problem?" The patient, in a hurry and stumbling voice said: "I can't.......... I can't miss her.......... I can't miss her at all"… Bul Bul asked: "Who is she that you can't miss?" He continued to repeat "I can't miss her……" and Bul Bul emphasised: "Who is she?"…. Finally the patient said: "Aziza". Bul Bul asked: "Who is this Aziza? Is she your sister or your daughter or what?" The patient replied: "She is the only person I love and I never relax". Bul Bul looked at Hakeem Hashim, who in turn, looked at him in a gesture of hope and success for him to be able to diagnose the wicked disease which was hiding in the heart of the patient. Hakeem Hashim said: "Bul Bul my Son! Your patient is suffering from love, and his treatment is with himself. He has to search for Aziza who is causing him to lose weight and should marry her as that is the only solution to his problem."

The method which Bul Bul applied to diagnose his patient – as his first test – made Hakeem Hashim very hopeful and he congratulated Bul Bul and told him: "Bul Bul! Your mother will be very happy to hear your cleverness and your know-how in your new career which will enable you to earn your living. I am sure that this will be one of the means, which will lessen your misery, which you had in the past. Now go and tell your mother this good news because she alone deserves to know about your success in your career". With much joy, Bul Bul kissed the hand of Hakeem Hashim as a token of his thanks for teaching him that knowledge. He then went to inform his mother.

KURNA KURNAZAKKOSH

You will recall that Hakeem Hashim was a healer who knew different kinds of healing, and that of his kind of healing was his ability to give orders to inanimate objects such as chairs, tables, household utensils and other things. Hakeem Hashim never applied this knowledge haphazardly but only when there was a real need for its application and on very limited measure. One day when Hakeem Hashim was teaching Bul Bul more of his knowledge he taught him this art of instructing the inanimate objects. He told him that in this field one needs to have a strong heart and that there is a special language that is used to do the job. He wanted to show Bul Bul an example of this work and he told him: "Bring me that pot of water". Bul Bul did as he was told to do, and he brought it, Hakeem Hashim threw it on the ground. It broke up into pieces and Hakeem Hashim said: "now I am showing you the power and the miracle of this knowledge. Look at these pieces of pot carefully and you will see the miracles which I have told you". Hakeem Hashim began to look at the pieces of the pot with fierce eyes while saying words in a whisper using the language which Bul Bul never heard before. He rise his arms pointing to the object stared at the pieces without winking his eyes. The pieces began to shake and came closer together and the pot began to reform itself until it regained its original shape. Bul Bul was puzzled and surprised with that miracle. If he did not see it himself he would not have believed any story about it. He picked up the pot and looked at it carefully to see if there was any part of it still broken, but he could not see any sign. He said to himself: "this is not a person to flirt with; he has much knowledge and deserves to be feared. I now believe his words when he told me that he is a healer and has much knowledge". Bul Bul became much interested in acquiring such knowledge and began to instruct different objects in the room to follow his commands. Every time he used this method and attempt to give orders to inanimate objects to obey him, nothing happened. He almost broke all the utensils in the house in his attempt to make them reform into their original shapes but in vain. This condition made Bul Bul's mother to worry as she saw things get broken without knowing who broke them. She told Hakeem Hashim about it and he told her: "you just remain quite, I know who breaks them and we shall get him. Just be patient".

After difficult training, Bul Bul was advised by Hakeem Hashim that it is unlawful to apply the knowledge of healing to harm people and other creatures. It is applied only for the benefit of those who seek treatment. He told Bul Bul: "It is our duty to heal people and not to harm them as other people who do not know the reality of healing. Our duty is to help people to lead happy life and not to deceive them as others do. Such people, my son Bul Bul, are not healers but are wicked people who cooperate with the devils in their deception. You have to remember, my son Bul Bul, that God is not on the side of the wicked as He had established in his holy book – Qur'aan. Also apostles of different religions teach us the same thing. "Do not be an isolator but be a real healer". Bul Bul nodded and promised to be as his teacher has advised him and will follow the right path and not the path of wickedness and hypocrisy.

THE HEAD SPEAKS

One day at nighttime, after finishing his routine work, Bul Bul felt very tired and became drowsy. He decided to go to bed but before he left the room where they used to exercise their work of healing, he remembered those actions of healing which Hakeem Hashim used when he broke the water pot and then brought it back to its original form. He was anxious that to try again in the hope that he might succeed and possess the power of knowledge like his teacher Hakeem Hashim. Without thought to know what power or ability Hakeem Hashim possessed which enabled him to perform such things, Bul Bul thought it were those sayings only which were the source of every thing. So he found it better to try it himself and perhaps he would succeed. He began to give orders to the different things, which were in the room such as the pots used for preparing drugs, chairs and other things. There was no sign of success though he tried hard to an extent that he protruded his eyes fiercely and raised his voice loudly. In the room, there was, among the things which they use in studying the healing, a skull of a human being, which was used for teaching Bul Bul the shape of the human head. Hakeem Hashim had it before for his own work. After trying all the things in the room in vain, Bul Bul decided to try these skull - perhaps it may respond.

He began to stare at it and pronounced the sayings, which he had heard from his teacher Hakeem Hashim. Soon after finishing the sayings, the skull moved a little from its position on the table and faced Bul Bul. He became very frightened and began to tremble in fear. His legs were shaking and he remained standing without moving a single step. He asked himself if the skull actually moved or was it merely his imagination! He thought that he was just dreaming. He decided to look at it carefully and went to where it was on the table and began to touch it with great fear. When he found that it had nothing, he held it without fear and turned it on all directions. He concluded that it did not move at all because he did not detect anything therein. He was convinced that it was no more than the same skull, which he touched every day. He brushed off his suspicion, as he believed that the art of healing does not agree with a timid heart, which cannot tolerate difficulties and problems of the patients. He thus ignored the skull and continued to attempt to give orders to the material things to obey him. He began to repeat the same sayings while he turned opposite the skull. When he finished the sayings he heard a loud voice calling him by his name "Bul Bul". He turned back in great fear and surprise and looked everywhere for one who called him but could not see anybody. His heart began to beat quickly and he asked in a frightened voice: "Who are you calling me?" There was no reply! He felt it better to go out of the room and go to sleep. He began to move slowly in tiptoe and suddenly he heard again the frightening voice calling him "Bul Bul". Bul Bul became more frightened and he could not control his shaking legs. He began to sweat all over his body. He protruded his eyes like a person who feels that he is being followed by someone whom he does not know in darkness. He asked in a trembling voice, pretending not to be afraid while in fact fear had spread all over his body turn foot to head. He asked: "If you who are calling me have any business with me, I see it is better for you to appear openly so that we can see each other". At that time Bul Bul was wet with sweat. The voice replied while laughing loudly: "Ha! Ha! Haa! I am here in front of you Oh! Bul Bul". Bul Bul inquired: "Why can I not see you if you are in front of me?" He was replied: "I can see you: Bul Bul attempted to speak with harshness: "Come on! Show up yourself! Why do you hide yourself? Are you afraid of me?" The voice replied to him:" It is a woman who becomes afraid. Will you have courage to meet me if I show up myself? O! Bul Bul?" You should not yourself act as a woman because of the fear which you have". Bul Bul swallowed the saliva he had collected in his mouth because of fear, and then said: "Come! Who do you think is afraid of a voice of a person who is not seen? The voice replied: "If that is so, then get ready for, I am coming".

Bul Bul began to hear trilling sounds behind him, and when he turned back he saw the skull had lifted up and hanging in the space by itself and moving around. When he saw such strange thing, which he never expected, he could not resist and fell down on his stomach yelling loudly and foaming from his mouth and trembling. He hides his face with his hands. Hakeem Hashim was frightened by the yelling of Bul Bul where he was asleep, and when he woke up he could recognize Bul Bul's voice. He hurriedly rushed towards where the sound came from. He understood that it was coming from the room where they keep drugs. When he entered the room he saw Bul Bul still lying on his stomach, trembling with fear. He did not know the cause of all that. He went closer to him and began to call him while touching his shoulders. When Bul Bul felt somebody was touching his shoulders and calling him, he became more frightened and yelled more in uncontrollable trembling; saying: "OH MY GOD! It is enough! – I repent Oh! Master! I shall never play with you again; I will never be rude with you again! Please pardon me my fellow creature. Do not pull out my soul!" Hakeem Hashim became more puzzled with such events because until that moment he did not know anything and did not see the skull, which was hanging in the space. He told Bul Bul: "stand up so that I can ask you. I am Hashim". When Bul Bul heard the name of his teacher Hakeem Hashim, he became a little relaxed and breathed slowly and began to raise his head slowly in great fear because he was not yet sure whether a person who touched his shoulders was really Hakeem Hashim. He hides his face with his hands while peeping through the openings of his fingers. When he was convinced that it was Hakeem Hashim who touched his shoulders, he embraced him and hugged him hard out of the fear he had and was wet with sweat. Hakeem Hashim asked him: "What happened to you this night my son Bul Bul? I see you in this state of confusion and fear!" Bul Bul in a state of great fear was stammering like a person who had lost his sanity: "Head! Head!" Hakeem Hashim asked: "Head?" and Bul Bul replied: "Yes! Your head". Hakeem Hashim inquired: "What is wrong with my head?" Bul Bul said: "It speaks!" Hakeem Hashim was surprised and stared at Bul Bul and asked him: "Do you not know all these days that my head speaks?" Bul Bul was all this time looking not at Hakeem Hashim but searching every corner in the space and then asked Hakeem Hashim: "Why did you not tell me that it speaks?" Hakeem Hashim became more confused and asked him: "Does not your head speak?" And Bul Bul replied: "I do not have one". Hakeem Hashim asked: "What? Don't you have one?" What is this one which speaks now?" "Whose head is it?" Pointing his finger at Bul Bul's head Bul Bul replied: "This is mine". Hakeem Hashim inquired: "Why then do you say you don't have one?" Bul Bul said: "I do not have like yours". Hakeem Hashim asked: "What is extra in mine?" Bul Bul replied: "yours speaks".

Hakeem Hashim felt that Bul Bul was trying to joke with him and hold him: "Listen Bul Bul! This is not the moment of making jokes" Bul Bul replied: "What I am telling you is true, my teacher, it is not a joke". Hakeem Hashim told him: "If it is not a joke, then what is it? Are you getting mad?" You speak something which I cannot understand!... Head... Head speaks... Are these the words spoken by a sane person?" Bul Bul told Hakeem Hashim: "Okay! I shall explain to you everything that happened. When you left me here, I continued with my work until I finished everything, but before I left, I was tempted to pronounce the sayings which you read to me that day when you were instructing the objects in this room to do what you wanted them to do." Hakeem Hashim was standing with his back facing the skull, which was still hanging in the space listening to the explanation of Bul Bul. Hakeem Hashim stretched his hand to Bul Bul indicating to him to stand up. When Bul Bul stood up he continued to explain to Hakeem Hashim what had happened which caused him to be in a condition in which he saw him. "When I was trying everything in this room to obey my instructions, I saw that none responded. Finally I found it worthwhile to approach the skull which you use for the drugs. While I was trying to commanded it like you did, I suddenly heard the voice calling me by my name".

When Bul Bul was relating history and when he reached the stage of pronouncing those sayings, the skull which was in the space behind Hakeem Hashim began to get down slowly towards the back of Hakeem Hashim until it reached very near his shoulder facing Bul Bul's face. When Bul Bul saw it, he became tongue-tied and opened his mouth and eyes in confusion, and suddenly he chanted, saying: "Look, it is coming towards me ... stop it.... It is behind you Hakeem Hashim. It is coming to me". He began to retreat step by step. Hakeem Hashim turned back to look and he saw the skull in the space behind him. He also became confused for what he saw but he understood later on what made the skull do as it did. He burst into laughter and laughed loudly without being able to control himself, while looking at Bul Bul at the same time. He held his stomach to ease the pain of his laughter. Bul Bul's fear disappeared abruptly when he saw Hakeem Hashim laughing in such a way. Hakeem Hashim stretched his hand and touched the skull and approached Bul Bul and told him: "Bul Bul, my son! Surely I shall never forget today's incident, though to me nothing is new but it rarely happens. I do not blame you at all for all that you have been saying and doing which initially confused me and made me think that you were kidding with me. You could not help being afraid, as it is not surprising for a person to lose his heart because of fear as a result of facing such a frightening incident. But in the course of our work we encounter events like these. The big difference existing between us and other healers who apply such things to harm people is that to us such a usage is prohibited. Never agree to cause death to anyone or to harm anybody for the sake of earning money which when you die you will leave it in this material world. This should be a warning to you that a matter which you have not been asked to do you should not do it. Notwithstanding that, we have really derived great benefit, as from this day I believe that you shall never do things you wre not taught to do except when it is really needed. It is said that a person learns or understands more through his mistakes. Since you are interested to know how to give instructions to inanimate objects to obey you, it was my intention of training you with this art. I think it is better for us to go to sleep because it is dead night now, and you need to rest. Tomorrow, God willing, after coming back from the mosque in the morning, you should remind me. Let us go to sleep. Bul Bul and Hakeem Hashim left the room and went to bed.

POISON IN THE HANDS
OF A LOVER

fter the morning prayers on the next day, Bul Bul reminded Hakeem Hashim on their way back from the mosque, the promise he gave him last night, because he very much wanted to know about the art of healing. When they reached home, Bul Bul, as was his habit, which his late father taught him to greet his parents every morning, went to greet his mother. He kissed her hands and told her "Good morning Mother". His mother returned the greeting by kissing his hand and saying "Good morning Son. Although he went with Hakeem Hashim to the mosque, he used to greet him when they reached home. After having breakfast which was prepared by Bul Bul's mother, they thanked God, and Hakeem Hashim, as he wanted to do, prayed and said: "Oh God whom we trust, God who has no associate, God who distributed justice equally to all your servants and your judgment is justified without any hindrance or favour, this bounty which you provide for us everyday and every hour comes to us out of your grace for us – your creatures. Accept our sincere thanks and guide us to the path, which is good for us, and protect us from the evils of our fellow creatures and save us from the wicked people. "You are alone who possess such ability and you have no partner" All of them said: "Amin"

Hakeem Hashim told Bul Bul that it was time for them to go to their work. They left and went to their room. When they reached there, Hakeem Hashim told Bul Bul: "I know that you did not sleep last night becaof what happened to you and also because you very much want to know." Bul Bul nodded and said: "Yes it is true". "The whole night I was awake and wanted to know". Hakeem Hashim continued: "I want you to know that this art of healing which I am teaching you is great – very very great, for although I am a stranger in these islands. I am very popular in different parts of the world, and I have spent much of life in studying this art. A day will come in your lifetime when you shall be proud and boastful because of the popularity, which you shall acquire for this art, which I am teaching you. Now, in continuing with our aim, you must know that anything which you instruct by using that language which I mentioned to you, such a thing will not only come closer to you and obey your orders, but it can, also speak words similar to a human being. For example, take this skull which you instructed and which stood up and spoke. With the help of this knowledge, which I shall teach you, it will be able to answer your questions of any kind, which you would wish to ask. "Come here so that I may show you an example". Hakeem Hashim moved near the table where the skull was kept. He lifted his right hand towards the skull. He shut his eyes and pronounced those strange words: "Kurna Kurnazakkosh, Kurna Kurnazakkosh Aetra Banda Hayata Ya Khuda". When he finished saying those words Hakeem Hashim lifted his hand up and the skull raised up and faced Hakeem Hashim. During this time when Hakeem Hashim was explaining Bul Bul, he remained quiet listening attentively and watching his teacher everything that he did.

After instructing the skull to float in the space Hakeem Hashim turned to Bul Bul and told him to go near him. When Bul Bul went near, Hakeem Hashim took off his ring from his last finger and gave it to him to wear it, which he did. The ring was made of black mineral (metal). It was neither of gold nor of silver nor of copper. There was a beautiful spot in the center and every time the ring is turned around, the spot changes its colour very attractive to the eyes. Hakeem Hashim asked Bul Bul: "How do you feel after wearing this ring?" And Bul Bul replied: "I feel all my body is hot, and my blood is circulating quickly". Hakeem Hashim sighed: "A Haaa! That is the sign that you may acquire the knowledge which you are seeking". He then told Bul Bul to look at the skull sternly; and Bul Bul did as he was told to do. Hakeem Hashim then told Bul Bul: "now ask the skull any questions you wish and it will answer you". Initially Bul Bul was confused as he did not know what to ask but after some thinking he felt he could ask some questions. His first question was: "Tell me your name!" The skull replied: "My name is Darham Khan". Bul Bul asked: "What were you doing when you were alive?" The skull replied: "In my country – India – I was a poet and a famous singer." In which century were you living?". The skull replied: "It is now four hundred and seventy years since I died". Bul Bul asked again: "What was the cause of your death?" The skull replied: "I was wronged by being poisoned". "Who gave you the poison?". The skull replied: "I was poisoned by some one who used to love me very much". Why should a person who loved be the cause of your death?" The skull replied: "Because of envy and hatred of other people who did not like to see us live happily. They were the ones who provoked my partner and made her the cause of my death". Bul Bul sighed! "My sympathies my friend! We humans are not good!" He continued to ask: "I hope it will not be difficult for you if I ask for something which I very much need!" Since you

were a famous poet during your lifetime, I would be very happy if
you read to me some of your poems which you composed when you
were alive". The skull replied: "Your request is granted. I composed
the following poem ten years before my death. Listen to it carefully
and memorize it lest you forget it. I hope it will be useful to you.
The poem bears great meaning. Seek its meaning to understand its
benefit. It is as follows: -

> "If death is a medicine
> To cure the pains
> It would have cured Hawa
> The mother of the universe
> For the loss of her husband
> When he committed a sin."

> "Should there come up
> He who values humanity
> I would grant him a gift
> Which people could not bear
> Bul Alas! They are lost
> And those remaining are nothing."

> "When I climb the tower
> My legs tremble
> When I enter the cave
> Fear surrounds me
> Where is the resort?
> Which is quite safe."

After finishing the poem, the skull asked Bul Bul: "Oh Bul Bul! Tell me your opinion about the language, which I have used. Will you be able to tell me the meaning of the poem? Bul Bul hesitated for a while and then said: "I am not a poet and I have no knowledge of poetry, but I understand that it is a great art for a person to use his brain to compose the language in a good style and produce the poem. The target and the real meaning of your poem is not what has been written and recited in the form of a poem. To answer your question, that I can answer the meaning of your poem – the answer is "I cannot, but I will try". The skull was very much pleased with what Bul Bul said. It was clear and meaningful. The skull was satisfied and allowed Bul Bul to try to explain the meaning of the poem. He told him to go ahead. Bul Bul began to explain (in an attempt) and said: "Ten years before your death, when you composed this poem, it makes me think that you lost some thing or some one or people who were dear to you – I mean some thing or some one who was very dear to you to an extent that you thought of deriving your soul for the furry of the loss which you got. But you realised and knew that doing that would not be the antidote to your furry. You knew that if that could be the antidote then it would have healed those who suffered before you who lost the roots of their lives. The skull said: "In fact you did not grasp the real meaning, but I congratulate you for your interpretation and I say that your brain is very very good Bul Bul. Now continue with the second and third verses". Bul Bul thought a little and after a while he began to explain the second verse and said: "The one you trusted did not respond to your trust: he cheated you very much – more than you expected, and after you discovered that he cheated you thought that you could not believe anybody else".

The skull said: "Bul Bul! I think between you and your teacher I must choose to thank one of you. - Go ahead Bul Bul". Bul Bul continued to explain the last verse, and said: "If you rush at the world, you will get what you do not want, and if you isolate yourself in this world, you will still find that there is no secrecy therein." The skull became very happy with the intelligence of Bul Bul and for his being able to interpret that poem, and it said: "Bul Bul: I don't know what I should give you for satisfying my quest. Were I still alive on this day! The interpretation which my fellow failed to give in that century has come today when I am no longer alive" Hakeem Hashim told Bul Bul: "I don't know how happy will your mother be when she hears the intelligence of her son who knew nothing before. I too congratulate you Bul Bul". After shaking hands with Bul Bul, Hakeem Hashim turned to the skull and told it: "Darham Khan, we have to leave you to take rest. We thank you for everything". Hakeem Hashim stretched his right hand towards the skull indicating to it to return to the table. It returned and rested on the table. Hakeem Hashim turned to Bul Bul and told him: "Bul Bul, that ring which I gave you is the one which has the power to give you instructions to do as I had shown you. Do not put it off under any circumstances. It should always remain on your finger. The knowledge, which you have acquired today, you always use it for good things and never use it for mischief. You should be a good healer to cure people and not to harm them". Bul Bul acknowledged all what he was told and promised to apply it without violating anything and said: "With your will, Oh God! Guide me and helpme".

POVERTY IS ONE'S OWN CHOICE

The next day was Friday, and as usual, Bul Bul woke up early in the morning and awoke Hakeem Hashim. They then left to perform their work. Hakeem Hashim attended the patients who had come for treatment and gave them the proper medicine. At 12 noon Bul Bul alerted Hakeem Hashim that it was time to go to the Mosque for Friday Prayers. They closed their work and left for the Mosque. After the prayers they went home and as usual Bul Bul went to greet his mother by kissing her hand and saying: "Good Day mother!" His mother replied: Good Day my son Bul Bul".

Bulbul invites a begger inside their home

Bul Bul's mother prepared the meals on the mat where they always have their meals. Before beginning to eat, the door was knocked from outside. Hakeem Hashim told Bul Bul that the person who was knocking was a weak person and what had brought him there was the need and the requirement of life – he said. "Go and open the door for him and welcome him in so that he may have his share of the provision with us". Bul Bul went to open the door, and he saw an old man who told him in a voice of a needy person: "My son! You see my condition. Problems of life make me wonder in the streets in search of those who may sympathise with me and give me something to fill my stomach – which troubles all the creatures. Help me my son! And God will help you". Bul Bul felt very sorry with the old man who was hungry. He said to himself that hunger is not sympathetic with any creature. He told him: "welcome my elder! Get in, because provision is not human's possession but God's. It is God who provides us to eat and to help one another. Come in my elder!". The old man raised his hands up and prayed: "Oh my Lord! Lord of all creatures! For quite a number of years I am in a state of starvation, and all these day I roam about seeking food to keep me alive. I have never come across anybody who welcomed me inside his house when I knock his door except today. Oh my Lord! Your will is always a marvel to your creatures".

He entered the house and was well received by Hakeem Hashim and Bul Bul's mother. He was welcomed to the mat where the food was waiting. He asked for God's blessings and began to eat with his hosts. After the meals, he again raised his hands up and thanked God and prayed: "Oh my lord! By your grace and mercy which are abundant in this world, grant these people everything which is good for them and grant them abundant sympathies so that they continue to help those in need who need help". All of them unanimously said "Amin". Hakeem Hashim also raised his hands up and prayed for the old man and said: "Oh Lord of justice! Your will is neither irresistible nor changeable. You never deprive anyone, and what you provide and you desist is your own will. My lord! Help him, your creature and remove him from his suffering and problems of seeking his provisions. Provide him with sufficient provisions so that he may help himself and stop roaming around begging from people who understand his problems and those who do not provide him with your mercy and your provisions – Oh my lord!".

When the old man heard the prayers, which Hakeem Hashim prayed for him, he burst into tears. He was so much moved to hear for the first time someone praying for him. Hakeem Hashim asked Bul Bul to bring ten rupees from their funds and Bul Bul brought the money. Hakeem Hashim told him to give it to the old man, which he did. The old man received money in a pleasant surprise. He was full of joy for the generosity of his hosts. Hakeem Hashim told the old man: "My dear Sir! God does not minus money and does not send down to his creature a basket of fruit. He shows the way and helps those who wish to help themselves. Begging will never remove your problems of poverty. Take these ten rupees and when you leave here go to the market. There you will see a man who is dark in colour wearing a dish-dasha and a fez cap. He has beard mixed white and black. Go to him and give him the ten rupees and tell him these words: "Life is sweet and I long for it". He will reply to you: "It is very easy if you are able to work for it with perseverance". He will take the money and will give you a sheep. You should take the sheep and go to the butcheries. There you should look carefully for a shop which has no meat but the owner has hung three tails of either the goats or the sheep. Approach the owner and tell him these words: "Trust in God; He is not stupid". He will reply to you: "He who is meant to be chaste will never be unchaste". When he replies to you like that, then give him the goat and he will give you thirty rupees. Take the money and go to *Mchangani* village where they sell dates. Buy one package of dates for any price and take it to the Friday Mosque. Cut the package and make small packages wrapped in papers and sell each package for half a rupee. Business will go smoothly but remember one thing which is very important: "At sunset, before the call for evening prayers is proclaimed, you should stop your business whether or not you have finished selling the dates. If anything remains unsold, give it to the guardian of the mosque and tell him to distribute it to the people who come for prayers. You will find that, after selling the dates, you have enough money. This should be your vocation to help you earn your living. You should buy dates every day and sell it in retail – if you sell all of it, that is better for you and if some of it remains unsold, you should get it distributed to those who come to say their prayers in the mosque. I hope you have understood everything that I have told you, and I presume that you will do it without neglect.

The old man who was listening to Hakeem Hashim attentively said that he had understood all the instructions and promised to do accordingly. He bade farewell and thanked his hosts for everything which was done to him. He left and went away.

After the old man had gone, Bul Bul asked Hakeem Hashim the aim of his telling the old man all that he had told him. Hakeem

Hashim knew that not only Bul Bul would like to know but also his mother the story behind his long speech to the old man. Hakeem Hashim then said: "Poverty is a bitter thing and it is very difficult to remove it. The problem is to determine who is poorer, what poverty really means! You will see that he who has nothing calls himself poor in front of one who has a little. He who has one hundred calls himself poor before one who has a thousand, and he who has a thousand calls himself poor before one who has one hundred thousand, and so on. Now the question is 'who is poor?'. You will find that the poor is the one who does not want to be in difficulties but at the same time he is not ready to trial to earn his living. Such a lazy person calls himself poor and claims to have nothing. This old man wishes to lead a happy life but he lacks the resources. You have to bear in mind that although he is poor, he is not begging for money. When he came to us he was hungry, and he came to ask for food. So giving him ten rupees and telling him to go to the first person who happen to be my friend who once came to me with his problems and I healed him. After his problems were over, he was greatly surprised to see that I charged him very little, I told him: 'I always help those who are in difficulties and who are poor. I know that he stays the whole day under the sun expecting to get a goat or a sheep to sell. Some days he gets and some days he does not get. Since his income is little and is not stable, I considered his condition and charged him little. I also told him the very words which I told the old man to tell him that: "Life is sweet and everyone longs for it and it is very easy to realise it only if one is ready to toil for it through perseverance and endurance. He did not understand the inner meaning of these words and asked me to explain to him. I told him that if a human being is satisfied with what he gets, whether big or small – much or little, and considers the conditions of other people, there is no doubt that God will be generous to such a pand will open for him the channels of more prosperity. Consequently, from that day, he swore to me and vowed that he will help everyone who is in difficulties according to his ability. When the old man goes to him, he will know that he came from me because of the saying which I told him. That will be my identification, and he will give him a sheep for his ten rupees although the sheep will command a price of thirty rupees.

When I told him to go to the butcher who displays the tails of goats or sheep, it is because I also know that man. He is generous but very lazy and does not want to trouble himself to improve his business. He only waits for something to be sent to his shop to buy it. He never goes to fetch it. So I knew that when the old man sends his sheep he will buy it.

When Bul Bul saw that Hakeem Hashim remained silent, he asked him: "But I remember you told that when he reaches the shop he should say: "Trust in God: He is not stupid" and that he will be replied: "He who is meant to be chaste will not be unchaste". 'Why did you not explain to us about this saying?' Hakeem Hashim replied to Bul Bul: "The meaning of that saying is that; one day I went to this man to get meat from him, and when I reached his shop I did not see anything except the three tails of sheep hanging. I asked him why all the butcheries of his colleagues were full of meat and only his butchery was empty?" and he replied: "God gives sustenance to his servant wherever he is; even the insect who lives in the stone which has no hole for breathing or through anything can penetrate.

Such an insect gets it provision therein". Thus I told him that you should trust in God; He is not stupid; and he told me: "He who is meant to be chaste cannot be unchaste".

Bul Bul further asked: "How about the package of dates; why did you tell him that at sunset he should stop selling dates and should distribute what remains unsold to those who come to the mosque for prayers?" Hakeem Hashim replied to him: "Yes! I told him so because I know that there is greed and speculation in any business. Every time you expect to sell more and more and gain much more money; and as our elders have said that: "Much greed cause death". Thus I was afraid that greed should not dominate him to an extent if forgetting to worship his lord at the time of prayers. So I told him to close his shop at sunset whether he sold all his stock of dates or not and that if there remains anything unsold, he should distribute it as alms to those who come to say their prayers in the mosque. That is the principle that as you give, God will give you more. I said that because the price of the package of dates is such that even if only half of it is sold, still there will be much profit. Thus, he will not incur any losses by distributing what remains unsold as alms". Bul Bul and his mother were satisfied with the explanation of Hakeem Hashim regarding the story of Hakeem Hashim and the poor man.

THE HOUSE OF WONDERS

One day Bul Bul went to the market and after buying all that he needed, he went to buy bread for their lunch. He asked for hot breads, but before he paid money, he felt someone was touching his shoulder. He turned back to see who was touching him, and surprisingly he saw a girl who was wearing a veil who covered all her body. Nothing was visible except part of her face where there are eyes. It was impossible to guess who she was. She asked Bul Bul: "I beg your pardon! I think I am not mistaken! Are you Bul Bul the student of the healer?" Bul Bul replied: "Yes Madam, I am he". The girl said: "Again I repeat my apologies; but if you will not mind, I would request you to go to that corner where there is some privacy so that we can talk. I want to tell you why I asked you if you were Bul Bul". Bul Bul agreed to follow her to the side of the road and the girl began to say: "Bul Bul, you will really be surprised to see that I talked to you and I recognised you although we do not know each other. There is a reason for that. I have been going around throughout this day trying to come to your house and luckily, when I approached this bakery I heard someone greeting you and mentioning your name. According to the description I was given about you I recognised you when I looked at you that you are the very person I was looking for. However I was not satisfied until I asked you whether you were the Bul Bul I wanted to see. The reason of my coming to you is that I have an important and very urgent errand which comes a little far. It is from a particular house where

you are requested to go. I know that it is very difficult for you to
accept my words first without hesitation. You may even suspect that
I am a wicked person who perhaps wishes to harm you or to lead you
to dangers. I request you to believe me and not to have any doubts
or suspicion on me. I have no bad intentions against you, and as I
told you before, I am only a messenger. The one who needs you is
still to be seen. Please give me your decision".

After listening to the long explanation of the girl, Bul Bul could
not say anything. He was thinking what to reply. He thought to
himself: "Is what this girl tells me true or false? How could I agree
and believe all that she told me? Should I follow her or not? Perhaps
she is right and if I refuse to follow her, she will consider me stupid.
That will be a shame on me. Nevertheless my heart is still hesitant
because although this girl's eyes shows truthfulness, I have not yet
seen her countenance. I do not know how she looks like". Finally
Bul Bul told the girl: "Madam! In fact all my silence I was talking
to myself because I do not know whether or not I should believe
your words. This was my problem. Nevertheless, it may be that you
are telling the truth, and I have decided to agree to follow you to
where you tell me that I am needed, but before I follow you, I have
one condition". The girl asked what condition it was and Bul Bul
said: "You should lift your veil from your face so that I can see you,
because until this moment I do not know how you look like, and if
I do not see your face, I will not be able to recognise you when we
meet again. If I see your shape, then undoubtedly I shall recognise
you even in the sleep". Without uttering a word the girl unveiled her
face for Bul Bul to see her. He became tongue-tied at the beauty of
the girl. He could not hide his feelings to see the beauty which was

hidden by the veil. He told her: "Thank you very much Madam. I am now satisfied and I have decided to believe everything which you said and I agree to come with you. Now please go in front of me while I follow behind".

After walking for about fifteen minutes, Bul Bul found himself in a place where there was a big house. It was situated far from other houses and was of ancient architecture. Its door is big with balls/beads made of copper. It has beautiful designs of leaves and flowers on its sides and on the top there are other beautiful designs. Besides the designs on the top is the Qur'aanic verse from the chapter "*INNAH FATAHNA*". It really added the beauty of the house – such doors are common in the islands of Zanzibar.

When they reached at the door, the girl knocked it, and the door was opened after a short while by another girl who was taller than her friend. She was wearing a long gown, which had black flowers. The cloth was yellowish. She wrapped her head with a muslin called '*Kanga*' and her hairs could not be seen – only her face was seen. After opening the door and seeing her friend who went with him, nobody spoke to another. The girl who was inside, nevertheless showed interest to look outside as if looking for someone or something. Bul Bul said that he thought the girl was looking at him and to make sure whether I have come or not, or whether the girl who was sent to fetch me had found me or not. The girl who I accompanied got in first and welcomed me in, and I followed her inside the house. When I approached the girl who opened the door for us, I felt that her face was not normal. She either had colds or was crying very much or her eyes were paining. However I could not help suspect everything which surprised me. The inside of the house was quite different from the outside. From the outside door and all over, Arabian carpets were heavily spread. On every wall was a big copper chest glittering and shining. The lights were tubes placed in bowels made of pleasant crystals fixed on the walls. Every corner you look will please you. Surely those who look at this house must be people who take great care and make every effort to keep it clean.

Bul Bul was welcomed and was asked to sit down on the chair and he did sit on the chair to wait for the instructions of his hosts. The girl who brought Bul Bul disappeared and he never knew where she went. The one who opened the door for them went upstairs towards the top floors, and after a while she came back and told Bul Bul that he was wanted upstairs. Without saying anything Bul Bul followed up to the top floor. He went through many rooms until he reached a place which looked as a guest room. The girl asked him to wait there. The girl then proceeded further to the door which had a beautiful curtain from top to bottom. The cloth of the curtain was very attractive to the eyes. Bul Bul knew that it was not a local cloth. It must have been brought from abroad. While waiting at the reception room, Bul Bul looked here and there and thought: "These people must be very prosperous. Everything which I have so far seen costs a lot of money". He found himself in the sea in which he could not swim. Suddenly the door behind the curtain opened and a different girl came out wearing a black long gown touching the ground. One could not even know whether or not she was wearing sandals. Her feet could not be seen. She was holding a cloth in her hands. She combed her hairs beautifully though she had a black transparent scarf which made her hairs and her long neck visible. She was lean and a little tall. Her complexion was a mixture of white and brown. Her eyes were sympathetic which beautified her face and had a black spot near her mouth on the right-hand side. In fact she was quite beautiful with a particular and peculiar features. Anyone who will looks at her cannot afford not to be moved in his heart.

Narima invite Bulbul in her father's room

She approached Bul Bul who was standing at that time as a sign of his respect for her. Behind her was that girl who opened the door for them when they arrived and besides her was another woman who had signs of old age but she was not old. The lady asked Bul Bul to sit down where he was and all of them took their seats nearly. The lady said: "I thank you very very much Bul Bul for accepting my call to come to our home. In fact all of us here ask for your forgiveness for wasting your time. Allow me to introduce you to my fellow ladies who are with me here. My name is Namira and this old lady you see here is my mother, and this young lady is called Salma and the girl who came to take you home is Salma's younger sister. She is called Muzna. The problem and the calamity which has afflicted us in our house cannot be explained, but after remaining quiet for the last seven days during which period we have been thinking how to go about it or what to do about it, knowing that all of us are women in this house, we could not decide what to do. However, when we heard about you and your knowledge of healing, we decided to ask you to come to us. We are not sure if what we called you for, you will manage to deal with or not, but we found that it was better to take our chance than to remain quiet. Thus, today in the morning we resolved to do something perchance it would help us out of this problem and rid us of this calamity". Bul Bul asked: "I thank you all for giving me this honour, but I see it is better, first of all, to explain to me in detail, what really is your problem and what assistance you require from me". Namira asked Bul Bul to follow him to the room from which they came. Bul Bul got up and followed the lady to the room. When he entered the room, he became puzzled – such a puzzle he had never experienced before. What he saw therein were strange things which looked like a fairy tale and not the reality. What added to the wonders was the state of the room itself. Had he not seen it with his own eyes, he could not have believed any explanation about it. Grass was grown on the floor of the room similar to that grown in the garden or on special yards. The grass was grown with great expertise – smoothly laid down in such a way that if you see it you will think it just a green carpet. On all the walls up to the ceiling were creepers of different kinds with flowers of various colours pleasant to the eyes. The whole room looked beautiful. In fact it is the sight which is very rare in those days. Added to the creepers, the walls were ornamented with copper plates of different kinds, such as big copper trays, jugs made of silver and other things.

After looking at such wonderful ornaments, Bul Bul saw a bed in the center of the room. It was very big and was made of copper which was shining because of being cleaned every day. He nevertheless became very much frightened when he saw something resembling a human body on the bed. It was covered with a cloth from foot to head. Namira went to the bed and removed the cloth which had covered the body. Bul Bul was surprised because what he thought looked like a human body was an image of a male stone. He went closer to the bed to look at the image carefully. Namira with tears running from her eyes to her cheeks began to explain: "Bul Bul! This is my father! He has been in this condition – neither dead nor alive". We do not know what has caused him to like this. The sorrow, which has filled our hearts in this house, is very much – much more than you can imagine. Being women all of us do not know what to do. That is why we called you to exercise your know-how in your profession of healing which is most useful in our islands".

Bul Bul thought for a while and then said: "It is true, ladies, that the misery which has afflicted you is great. It is a very surprising and a strange calamity. I must be frank with you although it will be disappointing! My knowledge of these things is limited, as such things are God's will and his miracles or it may be they are caused by witchcraft. I am a healer of different kinds of diseases in the human body but I am not an expert in witchcraft. Therefore, if what has afflicted your father is God's decree, then there is no human being who can interfere with God's will. If however, the misfortune has been caused by human beings such as those I have mentioned to you, then it requires a highly experienced person to detect the cause. There is very little hope on my side to help you out of this misfortune which has afflicted your father. I find it worthwhile to explain the case to my teacher who taught me this knowledge. He is the man who has much knowledge and it may be that after coming here and examines your father, he may find a way to help you".

Bul Bul's suggestion aroused much hope to Namira and her mother together with her foster sister. They all agreed that Bul Bul should come again with his teacher.

KAMRAASHI'S WITCHCRAFT

After listening carefully from Bul Bul the story about Namira's father, Hakeem Hashim said with beaming face: "my son Bul Bul, this is the greatest opportunity which comes to me in my life. It is the opportunity which I have never had since I finished my studies in healing. Accept what I tell you that this is a human act and not God's decree. The most important thing now is to get more information about this man. His abode, how he used to live, things which he liked to do and many other things which will help us to detect the beginning of diagnosis and the way to help him regain his life. I feel that it is better for us to go and see this man who turned into a stone this afternoon.

Bul Bul and his teacher went to the house of lady Namira, and on arrival they were received with great respect and honour. They were kept in a court in the top floor. After a short while, Namira her mother entered the court where Bul Bul and his teacher were waiting. After greeting each other, Bul Bul introduced Hakeem Hashim to Namira and her mother and said: "Excuse me ladies – I have to introduce you to Hakeem Hashim, who is the foundation of my knowledge. All that I know comes out of his efforts and his blessings". Hakeem Hashim also said: "It is a great honour to me, my ladies, to give us your confidence and belief that perchance your misery may disappear". Namira on her side replied and said: "We presume that Bul Bul has told you everything about our problem". Hakeem Hashim replied: "Yes, Madam! Bul Bul told me everything;

and that is why I hurried up to come because this incident or misfortune which was afflicted you has aroused my curiosity to know what has caused it, but I believe that there is a human hand in it and it is not God's decree: although it is God who is able to do whatever the wills without any hindrance. There are, however, human beings that can abuse their abilities. I would request to be allowed to see the image. Namira took Mr. Hashim inside the room and pointed her on the figure lying on the bed. On entering the room Mr. Hashim observed one thing which striked his mind. He smelt the smell was filled the room. He suddenly stopped and began to trace the source of the smell and said: "It seems that last night or even before this room was fumed with *Ud* of a special kind or sticks or dry leaves. Is there anybody who knows about this?" Namira's mother replied in a surprise, thinking how Mr. Hashim could recognise the *Ud* or other things, which he mentioned which were used to fume the room the previous night. She said: "It is true Mister; yesterday but everyday since my husband has come back from his business trip we fume the room with *Ud*, which he brought from abroad where he usually travelled.

Then Mr. Hashim was surprised when he looked on the bed. He saw a figure lying on it covered completely, head to toe, with bed cover. He wanted to ask, but hesitated and just glared on the bed. When Namira saw Mr. Hashim took interest in what was lying on the bed, she said: "Since you are now here Mr. Hashim, you should also see what has happened to the figure on the bed which happened to be my father!" Namira then went to the bed and took the cover off. Mr. Hashim was shocked to what he has witnessed, as that was a figure of a man which has turned into stone.

I remember the day he turned into a stone he told me he wanted me to send him a fumigator and fire to try the new *Ud* which was given to him as gift from abroad where he goes for his business trips. When he put the *Ud* in the fumigator I saw that it produced much smoke – much more than the ordinary *Ud* which we use here. Its smell was also very strong and everything in the room was stuck with it.

Hakiym Hashim said: "If there is any of it remaining, then urgently and forthwith it should be thrown into the sea so that nobody can get it". Hakiym Hashim continued to say: "Lady Namira! Your father has been inflicted with severe witchcraft. The Ud, which he uses to burn to fume himself, was the charm itself, which made him unable to regain his condition. You have to thank God for enabling me to come here in this country, otherwise you would have to seek the healer who knows about this type of evil and its causes". He continued to say: "Your father travels to North Africa! Is it not so?" Namira replied: "Yes! It is there where he does his business. He takes goods from our country to sell them there – in North Africa countries, and from there he brings goods to sell them here". Hakiym Hashim said: "The Ud which he brought is prepared from the milk of the trees which grow in those countries and it is used for preparation of witchcraft drugs by evil people who harm others. Lady Namira, first of all I would like to tell you that in your wish to regain the condition of your father, it is essential that you explain to us in detail every thing about your father and how he used to lead his life; perhaps we could find a means by which we can reach our target. I mean we may detect the root of this misfortune while examining the life of your father". Namira then took them back to the living room and Namira began to explain: "As I said before, my father was a famous businessman in Northern Africa. He is known by the name of Sheikh Nahwandy but this is not his real name. It is his professional name by which people call him. His real name is Muhammed Farha. My father was a man who loved music. He used to play the *Ud* (Oriental made Guitar) cleverly which he learned in the Northern Africa. What I understand is that he used to be invited by his different friends to very big parties in those countries where he did business. Such parties that were held on different occasions so that he could entertain the guests and the hosts present there. During the party held by his sincere friend one day, as he told me, he played his Ud for about one hour until two strings of his Ud were cut – up but he continued to play without there being any interruption in the tune of the song he was playing. When he finished playing the song, all the people who were present applauded him for his cleverness, which he exhibited. Among those who were present there was a young girl called Kamraash; she went to my father and introduced herself to him, and after exchanging conversation she tried very much to persuade my father to follow her to her house. Although my father attempted very much to control his heart not to yield to the sudden and brief contact he had with her, the politeness and tricks shown by the girl overpowered his heart. He thought that she was a respectable woman and she was trying to invite him respectively.

**Narima shows Mustafa and Hakeem Hashim his
father laying on the bed as a stone figure**

My father could not refuse and was convinced that there was
nothing to be afraid of". "When my father travels, he usually takes
one month or even forty days, but since he knew that lady he took
some three months before returning home. He never told us; neither
did we know what made him stay longer there. When we asked
him, he told us that it was business and the new counterparts he has
got in touch with. My father's behaviour began to change and he
showed no interest to stay with us here in the house. He even began
to be strict and reproaching which was not his habit. These sudden
changes worried us very much. One day, after about two years since
he adopted his new style of life, he returned home as usual, and after
a rest of about two days, he called me to his room at early night.
When I entered his room he told me: "My daughter Namira! I have
called you tonight I want to tell you a secret, because I have now

grown old and death does not have an appointment when it comes, and life never bids farewell when it departs. Before I tell you this secret, I want your promise that you will not disclose it to anybody; because if your mother knows about it, it will affect her and cause her incurable feelings. Then he told me his story with Kamraash, and finally he told me that Kamraash insisted that he should marry her; but my father totally refused. He had no plans to marry another wife other than my mother. He thus left with an intention never to return to Kamaraash. That was his last trip, because three days after telling me his story he wanted the fumigator with fire in order to fumigate himself with the *Ud* which he brought, and that is the result which you had seen in front of you". Namira finished her story.

After listening carefully the entire story related by Namira as told by her father, Hakiym Hashim understood that what afflicted Sheikh Nahwandy must have come from Kamraash. He said: "Ladies! The work to try to bring back the condition of Sheikh Nahwandy is great and difficult, and it requires patience because it will take a very long time which cannot be predicted. But I and my student Bul Bul have agreed to face this problem of bringing Sheikh Nahwandy back to normal. The important thing is that we shall have to stop healing the people in these islands for the time being and travel to where your father used to trade, and we shall need money sufficient to enable us to travel up and down including other expenses". Namira, looking hopeful and happy replied: "You really do not know how much happy I am for telling us that you will take the responsibility of this kind. My father's life is more important than any amount of money. Just say how much you need and you will get it without any hesitation, and if during your stay there you shall need, I shall give you a letter to give it to one of the big merchants there who was trading with my father. Certainly you will get all kind of assistance which you may need".

Dhow "Mansura" on it's voyage in the high sea

THE FRIGHTENING STORM

After gathering their requirements for the journey, Bul Bul and his teacher made arrangements to set out in a Dhow which carries goods to different parts of the world. They left on a Thursday in an Omani Dhow called Mansura. The captain was a man of good reputation. He was so polite to the members of his crew to an extent that they listened to him and obeyed his orders without grumbling. At the outset, the wind was smooth and the Dhow sailed towards Mogadishu, which was the first port to anchor to unload mangrove poles, which came from Simba Uwanga. After three day's voyage, at about 2 a.m. after midnight, the crew on duty shouted and said: "Wake up! Wake up! The strong storm is coming from behind us". All the people in the Dhow got up and watched the storm. It was very frightening as the nightof the stars, which was pleasant, had turned into darkness and frightening. The black cloud covered the skies and the storm was blowing furiously and with such a speed that it caused the sea to be rough with very furious waves. When the captain saw the scene, he shouted: "Allahu Akbar! Allahu Akbar!" (God is great, God is great) "Brothers, this is the storm which sinks everything. Everyone should take care of himself".

The Dhow became the ground of people running here and there and people began to yell for fear of getting drowned. Seeing such a scene, Hakiym Hashim put off his turban and tore it into two parts and then tied the two parts together. He held the hand of Bul Bul and dragged him to the mast and told him: "It is better to get drowned or to be rescued rather than to jump into the sea where the hope for survival is very little. Let us tie up ourselves to the mast so that waves do not sweep us". Hurriedly they tied up themselves to the mast with the turban of Hakiym Hashim. The storm reached the Dhow and it began to swerve this side and that. The waves were high and caused panic and the storm became more speedy and made the Dhow bumps up and down. Much of the goods dropped in to the sea. The sail was torn to pieces and parts of the cloth thundered with the strong wind. The Formal, which sail is tighten with pole of the sail broke into two parts making such a big sound and both parts fell on the front part of the Dhow and tore up the board making a wide hole, which caused water to pour into the godown of the goods. When water filled the Dhow, the Dhow began to sink. There was no hope for survival. People who were missing were not known if they were drowned or still alive, but many were drowned, and only a few were alive. The situation continued for three hours. Only a few planks remained which helped to make the Dhow float. In spite of his stubbornness, Hakiym Hashim was equally dismayed and lost hope for survival. He remained the whole night praying for God's mercy to save them from the danger. Although they were still alive but since they tied themselves at the bottom of the mast they suffered much hardship of being hit by the big waves and they drank much seawater.

At dawn, the storm calmed down and the sea became normal but the Dhow was in a very bad condition. Many parts were broken and only a fraction of it was floating on the water. After breathing a long sigh of relief following the horrible night, which he will never forget in his life, Hakiym Hashim turned to Bul Bul to see his condition.

He was happy to see him alive and safe and still tying himself to the mast besides him. However, Bul Bul lost his consciousness, as when Hakiym Hashim called him several times, he remained silent. Hakiym Hashim became worried for Bul Bul's silence. He untied himself quickly and held Bul Bul so that he should not fall down. He laid him down and examines his condition and after making sure that he was alright except that only his consciousness was lost, Hakiym Hashim tried hard to help him regain his normal condition. He turned him upside down and massaged his ribs to make vomit the water, which he had drunk during the storm. In this way much water poured down from Bul Bul's mouth. Then he laid him on his back and pumped air through his mouth using his own mouth. Bul Bul began to turn his head to the left. Hakiym Hashim massaged his cheeks while at the same time calling him by his name. Bul Bul slowly began to open his eyes and closing them, like a person who is being forced to wake up from sound sleep. Soon he opened his eyes and began to look around and when he saw Hakiym Hashim he smiled and called him by his name: "Hakiym Hashim"; and tears were dropping from his eyes. Hakiym Hashim embraced Bul Bul and kissed him on the forehead while tears were pouring from his eyes too.

THE RESCUE

After helping Bul Bul and keeping at another place, Hakiym Hashim began to go around each part of the Dhow to check who was safe and who was lost. He began from the rear part where there was the helm. There he found two men on whom boxes and other heavy things had fallen upon them. When he attempted to help them thinking they were still alive, he discovered that they were already dead. Approaching the helm, he found the captain had also tied himself to the helm just as they had done to the mast. After untying him, he found that he was still alive but was very weak. Hakiym Hashim now found that he had two men whose conditions were not good and thought that he must get something by which to help them regain their health and strength. The most important things were food and water. He began to search every corner of the Dhow in the hope of getting some food but in vain. He went to Bul Bul and told him: "Bul Bul my son! If we do not get food and water, your conditions will be very bad, and also the strength, which I now have, will deteriorate. I have looked every where in search for food and water without success". Bul Bul told Hakiym Hashim: "I remember the captain was putting water in the water skin-made bag of the goat and hung it on the pillar which supported the roof over the helm and also had some dates and other fruits which he bought from the islands and kept them in his big box which is on the left side of the helm". When Hakiym Hashim heard the good news of food and water he was encouraged and began to look at the place where Bul Bul mentioned. He went to the helm to check if the water bag was still there or whether it had been washed away by the waves. Luckily he found it still securely tied up. He took it and went to the captain. He opened it and attempted to make the captain drink, and with great difficulty the water penetrated into the mouth of the captain. That was tantamount to be given a new life for after drinking the water he could open his eyes and looked at Hakiym Hashim. He made a sign indicating that he wanted more water. He then breathed and showed relaxation like a person who had walked a long distance and reached a resting point. After seeing the captain had gained his consciousness, Hakiym Hashim told him that he wanted to give water to his student Bul Bul who was also in a disturbed condition. The captain nodded. Hakiym Hashim went to Bul Bul to give him water and only after Bul Bul had drunk then Hakiym Hashim drank himself. Hakiym Hashim told Bul Bul that the condition of the captain is worse than his; he said: The situation we are in the high sea which does not show anything in the horizon, the captain is a very important person being the only one who knows about this sea. If only you could help yourself and moved to the rear of the Dhow at the helm where the captain is lying down". Bul Bul said that he could now move after some rest and after drinking water. He got up and began to move to the rear and Hakiym Hashim helped him till they reached the helm where the captain was lying. Bul Bul asked Hakiym Hashim if he found the captain's box, which contain food and Hakiym Hashim, said that he had not yet searched for it. When they looked at the place where it was kept, they did not find it. They thought that waves had swept it, but after looking at the boxes which fell on the two men who had died, Bul Bul could recognise the captain's box and told Hakiym Hashim their among those boxes, the biggest is the captain's. Hakiym Hashim went down where the boxes were and found it but he could not lift it because it was very heavy. He had no alternative but to apply his knowledge, which he did not favour to apply, except when it is very essential. He raised his hands up and prayed to the Al-mighty God within his soul and placed his hand on the box and suddenly the box moved to the place he wanted it to be. It went to its usual place where the captain used to keep it. Hakiym Hashim went to where the boxes were, and seeing that it was locked with a very big lock, he instructed the lock to unlock itself and it did unlock without the key. He then opened the box and took out a variety of foods; dates, oranges, coconuts and others. He gave Bul Bul some and told him to try to eat. He then cut an orange and went to the captain and squeezed its juice into his mouth. He cut three oranges and then took his own share and began to eat while looking at Bul Bul if he also was eating. He found him eating without any difficulty. After eating, Bul Bul became better and had regained his strength. Hakiym Hashim went to the captain to see if there has been any improvement after giving him the oranges. He found that he had opened his eyes wider. He asked him if he would try to sit down. He said he would try, and after helping him, he managed to sit down. Bul Bul asked the captain if he could attempt to eat some food and he told Bul Bul: "The sea is very brave Bul Bul; and if we do not try to eat, it will take our lives like those who are lost. Bring me what there is so that I may eat". Bul Bul brought near him the foods which he found in the captain's own box. He began to eat slowly; and after being fed up, he told Hakiym Hashim: "You have applied great skill to discover this food" and Hakiym Hashim told him: "If it were not you who bought it and kept it in the box, then all of us would have died of hunger, because we have brought it from your box". All of them were exhausted. After regaining his strength, the captain stood up and began to inspect his Dhow to see the damage and said: "The damage in the Dhow is not much, but the loss of many lives of the crew. There are not less than six dead bodies and to try to repair the Dhow by three of us will be a miracle, as there is also the job of emptying the water which has filled the Dhow and also to repair the broken shelter, besides that the sail is torn up though we have a spare one which, I am sure, is wet. Moreover, I do not know how we can get it when water has filled the Dhow! In fact our hope of leaving this place is very little".

Bul Bul drew Hakiym Hashim aside and told him: "I believe there is a way to make this Dhow float again and travel; why don't we help ourselves out of this problem and give hope of resuming his position as the captain of this Dhow?" Hakiym Hashim said: "I understand your thoughts Bul Bul, and I also had similar thoughts, and there is no other way. Let us share the job – you repair the shelter and I shall empty the water from the Dhow."

Hakiym Hashim and Bul Bul kneeled down and raised their hands up and prayed to God to answer their prayers and to bless what they were about to do. After finishing their prayers they stood up and stretched their hands towards everything, which they wanted to regain its original condition. The captain was just watching them quietly because they did not tell him anything about what they expected to do. He nevertheless was surprised to see them praying and while they were done they stood and stretched their hands. He became tongue – tied and just gazed at them. Suddenly the captain became very much frightened when he heard the sound similar to water boiling in the dish, and surprisingly he saw a big spring of the water which was in the Dhow gushing out with great force like the water, which flows from the ground. The water was running into the sea while the Dhow began to emerge on the sea. When the water was completely empty the Dhow was floating as usual. The captain was very much afraid because of the strange things he had seen with his own eyes. He remained quiet without uttering a word. He just watched what Bul Bul and Hakiym Hashim were doing. It was Bul Bul's turn now to repair the mast of the sail and bring it to its normal shape. When it fell down one part fell on the deck and made a hole through which the water blown by the waves penetrated. Part of it was still hanging up. Stretched his hand towards that part of the mast, which fell on the deck. Suddenly the log began rise up slowly and moved towards its normal position and joined the part, which remained hanging. Then Hakiym Hashim summoned the captain and asked him to show him where the spare sail was kept, and he told him that it was in the store down where equipments of the Dhow were kept. Hakiym Hashim again prayed while he shut his eyes and directed his face and hands up facing the heavens. When he finished praying he went to the opening where there was the stairs to go down and stretched his hands downwards, and suddenly sounds were heard – of the things pouring down and suddenly a parcel or a big wrapping came out of the opening and went up. (It was the sail). Hakiym Hashim gave instructions to the sail to unfold itself and to fix itself on its correct pole and it did as ordered. The wind was normal and the Dhow began to move.

The captain did not believe that Hakiym Hashim and Bul Bul were human beings. He thought they were *Jins* but he tried to convince his heart not to believe that they were *Jins*. Hakiym Hashim drew his attention by telling him: "Mr. Captain, the vessel is now in motion. Please go to the helm and direct it to where we are supposed to go". He stood up and hurried to the helm and began to look at the compass which was placed near the helm and directed the Dhow the right course.

THE JOURNEY TO MOROCCO

After sailing for seven days – day and night, the Dhow reached the port of Djibouti, which is one of the ports near Somalia. They anchored there and bade farewell to the captain. The captain was very sorry to part with his friends with whom he became very intimate. He confirmed that he had never come across people like them throughout his travels and all his life as a captain. The good things they had done to him were like miracles, which he will never forget.

Hakiym Hashim and Bul Bul began their long journey to Morocco. From Djibouti they mounted camels along with other travellers and set off towards Omdurman – a town in the Sudan. When they reached Omdurman they looked for a vessel which could take them to Assyut traversing on the river Nile. Assyut is in Egypt. They set off from Omdurman and after a number of days they arrived in Assyut where they took rest for one day, and on the following day they continued with their journey towards Bengazi – one of the ports of Libya. From Bengazi they travelled to Tunis and upwards to Oran in Algeria. After two days rest in Oran, they left for Marakish in Morocco. Their journey from Djibouti to Marakish took them two months and 18 days.

Morocco is a very beautiful country. The dress for men is long white robe with a head cover stitched with the robe itself. Women use similar dress but hey cover their faces and only eyes can be seen. They use either black veils or of any other colour. They looked for a house to stay in and they got one for thirty rupees per week. Rents are higher there than at home in the islands where there are many things. They took rest for two days before they began to look for what they went there to seek. They went around in the town and tried to familiarise themselves with the natives and to learn their customs and habits.

THE INCIDENT OF THE SNAKE

One day Bul Bul went out during the morning hours to walk around, and preferred to take a walk in the country side to look at the farmers and to get an idea of how they cultivate, harvest and their other activities. Fortunately, when he arrived there he found the farmers were harvesting the grapes and packing them in the baskets. Men and women were busy in this harvesting work and were singing beautiful songs. Bul Bul was very much moved with the sweet voices and he sat under the tree listening to the songs. At noon he found it better to return home fearing that if he was late, Hakiym Hashim would be worried. As he was leaving that tree, he suddenly heard cries from the farmers shouting: "Kill it, cut its head!". When he looked at the direction from where the cries came, he found the farmers running away while at the same time throwing stones on the ground, and some were using sticks. Bul Bul became curious to know what was it that stones were thrown at and wanted to kill it? He thus went to the scene and there he found that it was a snake that they were killing. It had already bitten a girl on her foot. Thgirl was seriously injured and foam was pouring from here mouth because of the poison of the snake. The farmers could not help her. Bul Bul hurriedly went to the girl and tore part of her veil and with it he fastened her foot above the place which was bitten. He tightened the cloth very hard without sympathy. He then went to the place where different kinds of grass grew near the fields of the farmers. He picked the grass, which he needed and returned to the

81

girl quickly. He asked the male farmers to get him a knife and with it he pierced the place which was bitten by the snake and pressed to get the blood pour out. Blood came out and slipped on her leg to the ground. After pressing very hard, he wrapped the cloth downwards to the wound, and making sure that the poison had come out of the wound, he dressed the wound with the grass which he had brought. The farmers were merely watching what Bul Bul was doing. After a few minutes the girl began to open her eyes and the foam which was pouring from her mouth stopped. She looked at her fellow farmers. When they saw their friend who was shaking and foaming from her mouth had regained her normal condition became happy and shouted in rejoice. They embraced Bul Bul, kissed him on the face and hands and finally carried him on their shoulders and took him to the village singing and rejoicing for their friend's health. Also the girl was carried by her friends and brought to the village. When the people in the village heard the shouting, came out of their houses to see what was there. When the news spread throughout the village about how Bul Bul healed the girl, they all joined in the celebration till they reached the house of the village Head. When the village Head heard the shouting he came out of his house to inquire what had happened. The farmers told him everything about Bul Bul's activities to heal their colleague and to save her from death, which was imminent because of the poison of that bad snake. The farmers used to believe that if such a snake bites one, there was nothing else but death. There was, however, medicine for that but it required one who knew it and how to use it. Bul Bul was made the guest of honour and was highly respected by the farmers. The village Head, acting on behalf of the farmers welcomed Bul Bul and told him: "Oh

Bul Bul! Truly we your brethren the farmers give you our heartfelt thanks for the cleverness and goodwill you have shown to save the life of our colleague who would have been dead by now similar to many who have died of the poison of such snakes. There is nothing we can give you except to welcome you to our village and to consider you as one of us. Your name will remain immortal in our hearts and we shall pass this news to our children of the coming generations so that your name remains unforgotten".

Bul Bul was very happy for the honour heaped on him and told his friends: "I thank all of you members of this village. You have given me great honour. In fact, as a duty to humanity there is no need for thanks and recompense. The great recompense, which I ask from you, is to understand that there are still many such enemies who have poison. They are creatures like us, and as you have said that many who have died have been the victims of these enemies. If, however, you knew how to treat victims of such enemies, perhaps nobody would have died. So, what you actually need is how to save those who are attacked by snakes. Many of you have seen with your own eyes what I have done to save this girl, and it is time now you learn how to treat patients of this kind. Any poisonous snake when it bites a person puts its poison into the body through its teeth. You should understand that the snake is clever to know where to bite. It bites where it knows that its teeth will reach the veins through which blood passes so that its poison follows the blood throughout the body and when it reaches your heart you lose your life. It is not possible to remove the poison from your heart but it is possible to stop it from reaching the heart through the method which I applied by wrapping the place with a cloth or string or anything else which can tighten the leg or the hand or any other place in order to stop the poison from spreading with the blood to the heart. The next step is to remove the poison from the place, which was bitten by piercing the area and pressing it out. Then to get the medicine to cure the wound. I have used certain grass which has such medicine but any other anti-poison medicine which can heal the wound is enough".

The farmers agreed with Bul Bul in his speech regarding how to prevent poison of the snake from affecting the heart and how to cure the place bitten by the snake. They wished that they knew this before, as it would have saved many of their friends from death.

A STONE PERSON

Bul Bul bade farewell to the farmers and promised them that whenever he had time he would visit them. He hurriedly left the village of the farmers and made his way back home knowing that Hakiym Hashim would be very much worried by this time for his long delay, but because he was a stranger he lost his way and went to another place where he saw a beautiful house. It was a house similar to other houses in that country, which had no roof except a floor shelter. He stood a bit far to look and he found that there was a clean pavement in front of the house, and on the right-hand side was a hut for keeping animals. Inside the hut were sheep, goats and two camels. At the center of the pavement was a well.

After standing there for a while, he noticed that the place was very quiet. He did not see anybody coming out of the house or entering it. Bul Bul forgot that he was being late to return home and was anxious to know more about that house. He could not even answer himself what was the strange thing or unusual that made him go to that house. Perhaps it was because he lost his way and was hopeful that he might find someone to direct him the correct path. Bul Bul resolved, in the name of God, to go straight to the house, and when he reached, he approached the door, but before he called, he heard the voice of a woman crying quietly but in agony. Perhaps she had been crying for a long time. She was murmuring: Oh my son! What has happened to you? To whom should I go for help? Being alone, what should I do? Oh my lord! What trial is this which you have brought to me?" She continued to cry in agony. Bul Bul was confused and amazed wondering whether he should knock the door or should leave the place. But where should he go when he had lost his way! He had no alternative but to knock the door; though the owners must be people who had a misery. He thought that he also had a problem at that moment and without getting any help it would be difficult for him to know his way to town. He took courage and knocked the door, and suddenly the cry stopped. He then heard someone moving inside the house and then heard the sound of the door being opened. When the door was opened a woman of middle age in sound health with mixed hairs of white and black appeared. She had marks of running tears on her cheeks.

Bul Bul respectfully greeted the lady; but the lady, instead of returning the greeting, was excited and just looked at Bul Bul with her eyes wide-open as if she had seen a marvelous thing or even a miracle. She came out of the house and went near Bul Bul while looking at him sharply and examining him every where. When she approached very close, she said in a soft voice and very slowly: "What wonders do you show me Oh! My lord! Is it true what my eyes see or is it merely a dream?" She touched Bul Bul's cheeks and continued to say: "Are you a real human being and not a *Satan* or *Jin*?" Bul Bul replied: "Lady! I am a human being like you. I have no relation with a Satan or Jin". "Tell me lady! What surprises you like this and makes you stare at me and touch my cheeks?" "Before I knocked your door I heard a voice of a woman crying and saying words indicating that there is something which has befallen her son, but after you had opened door and saw me I feel as if you have seen something you had never seen before. Tell me lady! What is the reason for all this?" The lady did not tell Bul Bul anything but instead she held his hand and told him to follow her inside the house. Bul Bul did not hesitate but followed her into the house. When they reached inside the house, the lady took Bul Bul to the bed and showed him one who was lying thereon. When he saw who was on the bed, Bul Bul could not help holding his head and throwing himself down and said: "There is no God but Allah, even in this country?" "Poor young man!" In fact when Bul Bul looked at the young man who was on the bed, he found him a stone similar to Sheikh Nahwandy; his whole body was an image of a stone. The lady then said: "This is the third day my son is in this condition, and I do not know what misfortune has befallen him. To me it is a misery, which has come to me. "Were he dead I would have buried him and hold the mourning period, but in this condition, I cannot tell anybody about him, because instead of consoling my heart, people would find it a puzzle, and people of the whole town would pour into my house to see the miracle. But the most interesting thing is you my son who have come here! If I tell you, you will not believe me! I would request you to look at my son's face carefully and you will understand what I mean". Bul Bul got closer to the young man who turned into a stone and looked at his face carefully, and then turned to the lady in a surprise as if he was asking through the eyes without uttering a word. He looked again at the stone and then said: "Is this true or I am dreaming?" The lady replied: "If you are dreaming, then our dreams are similar". Bul Bul told the lady: "Please, my lady, tell me more about your son and everything which you remember to the time he changed into a stone; perhaps with the will of God we may find a way to help him out of this tragedy".

The lady began to tell Bul Bul about her son: "God has gifted me with only one son, who is this one you see here, who has turned into a stone. His name is Rasheed, and his father left me since Rasheed was a minor of three years. All the problems of bringing him up were mine alone. At that time I had no property, but my only asset was this land which God has granted us. I am a shrewd farmer, I did not admit a defeat by the world fate, and therefore I did not accept to remain poor and beg for assistance to bring up my son. I resolved to take up my hoe and cultivated the land and grew every kind of produce. By God's grace I harvested my yield to use for myself and to sell in order to get my other requirements of life. We used to eat, my son and myself, out of the sweat of my brow. I brought up Rasheed through that way of self-reliance, toil and perseverance for the problems and difficulties of life; but do not believe to be told that a farmer is poor or may die of hunger. Such a person is not a real farmer but is an enemy of the farmers.

When Rasheed attained the age of fifteen years began to think of life in the town, which is completely different from our life as farmers. Life in the town is expensive, and there are many temptations which one can afford and which he cannot afford. I tried to explain to Rasheed and to persuade him to abandon that silly idea of wishing to leave me alone, but all my efforts were in vain because he insisted upon resorting to town. He did not listen to my advice.

After much consideration I found that if I forced Rasheed to remain with me here, he may decide to run away from me once and for all, and I may not see him again. I thought that perhaps, God wished to teach him life and what the world means. So I allowed him to please himself with my permission. Rasheed left me and left with me sorrow and loneliness, which I cannot describe. Every time I thought of him, as you know that when the passion of motherhood strikes you it does not relax. I used to think what he eats, where he sleeps, perhaps he is being made to work like a slave etc. etc. Again, who will look after him when I am his mother and I am far from him! Different thoughts crossed my mind, and I had nothing to do except to pray for him that God protects him and me knowing that the prayer of the mother for her child is granted quickly by God. Since Rasheed left my house I did not hear any news about him, and I did not know if my son was still in this country or not. Also he was not interested to know whether his mother was still alive or not. For a period of seven years I did not see Rasheed.

He returned home since twenty days ago, but since he has changed and became a grown-up person, I could not recognize him immediately. My old age changed when I saw my son Rasheed. I embraced him with great affection and tears dropped from my eyes on his shoulders. I raised up my hands and thanked God for protecting my son and bringing him back to me. I felt I had grown younger again and I was careful to please my son Rasheed for most of his needs so that he should not run away again from me. I have been doing for him everything, which he needed, and I surrendered to him all my love like any good mother does to her beloved son. Rasheed was not only a son to me, but was also like a diamond which deserved constant care being a rare thing commanding great value. I did that for fear that he should not wish to leave me again in my old age. But all my efforts were a good for nothing job, for although he did not leave again, but what remained at home was not Rasheed but a stone which you see in front of you.

I remember very well that one day he told me he wanted my opinion regarding his wish to marry, and when I asked him if he had anybody in mind he replied yes he had. I demanded to know who she was and whose daughter but he just said that there is one girl he had in mind. I told him that when time comes to give my opinion I shall tell him. He understood that his reply did not please me, and he softened me with his sweet words, and then told me that the girl he wanted to marry was the daughter of Sheikh Bauman bin Qulesh. His daughter was very popular in this country similar to her father. Her name was Kamraash.

When Bul Bul heard the name of Kamraash being mentioned he inquired slowly and surprisingly: "Kamraash?" and he was told "Yes! Why my son, do you know this lady?" and he replied: "No, but I once heard this name being mentioned". Rasheed's mother continued to say: "I was not willing at all my son to marry Kamraash – daughter of Bauman bin Qulesh, because there is no one in this country who does not know the wickedness of this man and his bad activities. He is a famous sorcerer who has harmed many people. Every one avoids him because of his sorcery, except those who are wicked like him and those who wish to wrong others. Those are the ones who cooperate with him". Bul Bul said: "Why then did you not think that perhaps your son has been inflicted with the wickedness of Bauman bin Qulesh?" Rasheed's mother replied: "I do not think that is possible because since Rasheed told me about his wish to get married until he turned into a stone, he never left this house". Bul Bul said: "but lady! I would ask you to consider this! It is possible that Kamraash forced Rasheed to marry her against his will, but he could not tell you this secret for fear that if he marries a woman he does not love, you will understand that he has been forced to marry someone he did not love. Perhaps Rasheed knows that Bauman bin Qulesh is a great sorcerer, and for fear of being harmed, he could not refuse to marry Kamraash, it is also possible that he did not give his consent straight away but he demanded a respite so that he could come here and consult you or to persuade you to agree, and perhaps Kamraash had given Rasheed a limited time to come to you and to return to her, and if he did not return within that time she would harm him. Thus because you refused him permission to marry Kamraash, he could not convince you or force you, and because of his love for you – being the only son, his love was stronger than his fear of being harmed by Kamraash. He thus ignored their threats and followed your advice; and that is why he turned into a stone".

After she heard carefully the views of Bul Bul regarding his thinking of the cause of Rasheed's fate to turn into a stone, she felt that perhaps Bul Bul's reasoning was correct, and that could be how things exactly were, and she said; "My son! I think what you say is possible because it is easy for a man and his daughter to reach here with their sorcery and to harm him or anyone they would like to harm. By God, I now begin to see how things are. I begin to perceive the truth now. It is true that perhaps Rasheed did not want to marry Kamrash but he was afraid of being harmed, and perhaps not only he but also me, his mother. And perhaps that is why Rasheed did not go back to tell Kamrash anything as he had decided to accept what may come to him but could not leave out here alone for fear that those wicked persons should harm me. That is why he stayed with me so that he could see me every time. My poor son Rasheed! The wicked did not spare him!". Tears poured from her eyes.

Dear readers of this story, Let us stop to ask ourselves what made Rasheed's mother to be greatly surprised when she saw Bul Bul? And why did Bul Bul become tongue-tied when he saw the stone image of Rasheed? The reason for all this is because Bul Bul and Rasheed were young men who very much resembled each other. So much alike like twins. You will deny emphatically if you are told that they are not brothers and are not related to each other. The likeness of their shapes was what made Rasheed's mother to be surprised when she saw Bul Bul, and which made Bul Bul to be equally surprised when he saw the stone-image of Rasheed. The difference between them was so little, which does not accept the idea that they were not brothers.

BAUMAN BIN QULESH

Bulbul and Maalin Hashim in Rasheed's home

---

fter hearing the details from Rasheed's mother regarding her
son, Bul Bul found that he had discovered the way to detect
how Sheikh Nahwandy was turned into a stone similar to Rasheed.
He thought that although he was late to return to his teacher Hakiym
Hashim, he was sure that when he relates the story to his teacher,
he will be satisfied and pleased. He then told Rasheed's mother: "As
I told you before, that after explaining to me everything you know
regarding your son Rasheed, there may be a way to help him out of
this misery. I do not promise you much but I am hopeful that your
son Rasheed will regain his condition. I myself and my teacher, who
by now must be worried about my being late to return home, we
shall try our best to help you and to heal Rasheed to regain his life

as a real human being". Rasheed's mother said: "My son, although I feel that it is just a fantasy – something unlikely, but you make me hopeful and give my heart strength. It is not easy at all to appear some one who can counter Bauman's witchcraft". Bul Bul laughed and told Rasheed's mother: "There is nothing impossible, which has been done by a human being. What is difficult is that which has been willed by God; and remember, my lady, that God is always not with the wicked and those who are destructive. He is always with those who wish good things for others. So there is no doubt that God will be with us, and there is no harm which Bauman bin Qulesh can cause us, as God will protect us from his wickedness". Rasheed's mother replied: "God protects you from all wickedness, my son, but I have a fear about you, lest you also become a victim of what you do not expect. Please, my son, do not plunge into the torrents of the wicked people like these". Bul Bul told her: "Okay! I have heard, mother, but I feel it is better now to show me the way to the town, because I only came here after losing my way. God willing, tomorrow I shall come with my teacher to discuss how we can do to help Rasheed regain his life".

After reaching home late in the evening, he found Hakiym Hashim was furious for his being late to return home, and he rebuked Bul Bul very much. Seeing Hakiym Hashim in such a state of furry, Bul Bul told him all that he had seen and heard that day. After hearing the story Hakiym Hashim become happy and was equally surprised to know that there is another victim – Rasheed – who has entered in to the trap of Kamaraash and was turned in to a stone similar to Sheikh Nahwandy. When Hakiym Hashim was told by Bul Bul that he and Rasheed looked like twins and resembled one another so much that if one is told that there is no relation between them, he said: "My son, Bul Bul! God likes us very much, because the means by which the problem of reaching what we have come for, has come by itself. If you had not gone for a walk to the fields of the farmers, then all this would not have happened at all. Let us wake up early tomorrow, and immediately after saying our morning prayers we shall go to Rasheed's mother. Hakiym Hashim continued to say: "Bauman bin Qulesh and his daughter Kamraash are within our reach now, and they themselves will come to us before we go to them".

Rasheed turned into stone statue

After saying their morning prayers on the following day, Hakiym Hashim and Bul Bul collected their luggage and left towards Rasheed's mother. After walking for about one hour, they reached the house of Rasheed's mother. Hakiym Hashim said: "This place is so quiet and has beautiful scenery". Bul Bul knocked the

door, and Rasheed's mother opened the door, and seeing Bul Bul
with Hakiym Hashim, she welcomed them inside. They entered
the house and seated on the mat, which was spread specially for the
guests. Bul Bul apologised to Rasheed's mother for their arriving
too early in the morning. He said it was very important for them to
come early. He then introduced her to Hakiym Hashim and he also
told her that his name was Bul Bul, because he did not tell her his
name when they met the previous day. Rasheed's mother requested
them to take a rest while she went to prepare tea for them. Hakiym
Hashim told her: "Since you are going to prepare tea, it is better if
you allow us to enter the room to see your son and to begin doing
what we intend to do". She took them inside the room while she
went to prepare tea. When Hakiym Hashim went to the bed and
seeing the image of a human being which turned into a stone, he sat
down besides the image and looked at it for a long time, and then
said; 'It is a great misery for any parent to lose a young lad like this,
particularly he is the only child. Bul Bul, you did not come here of
your own by merely losing your way; No! It was God who brought
you here so that you could console this lady from her anxiety. It is
quite true that you and Rasheed look the same and there is no much
difference between you. It will be very difficult for anybody who
does not know you to differentiate between Bul Bul and Rasheed".

Hakiym Hashim opened his books and began to read page
after page; and finally he produced his pen and paper and began to
write. He wrote of charms and told Bul Bul to hang them, one on
each corner of the house in the outside compound. Bul Bul took
the charms and did as he was told by Hakiym Hashim. He hung
each one of them on the edge of the pole, which protruded in each

corner of the house. Hakiym Hashim wrote another two charms and stitched them in cloths with strings to hang them. He tied one of them on the right hand of the image of the stone of Rasheed's body and tied the other on Bul Bul: "God is the protector of those who have faith: From the depths of darkness he will lead them forth into light. Of those who reject faith the patrons are the evil ones. From light they will lead them forth into the depths of darkness. They will be companions of the fire, to dwell therein (forever)" (Baqra: 257). This revelation has the following meaning as translated by the scholars: - "God is the protector of those who believe him. But those who reject faith, their protectors are the Devils. They lead them from light to darkness. Those are the companions of fire to dwell therein for ever".

Rasheed's mother then told them that tea was ready, and they got out of the room to drink tea with bread made from whole wheat. When they had finished their breakfast, they thanked God for the blessings he granted them that day. Hakiym Hashim told Rasheed's mother and said: "Lady! This misery which has inflicted your son comes from the wickedness of Bauman bin Qulesh, who is a very great sorcerer according to what I have heard about him. He never hesitates to harm anyone who attempts to interfere in his affairs particularly when he knows that there is someone who attempts to hinder his wickedness. He will do everything possible to destroy such a person. This is the habit of every sorcerer and wicked. They never hesitate to destroy anybody but on the contrary they become furious if others interrupt their wickedness.

There is no permanent wickedness in this life; everything begun by human beings has its end. God's punishment is very great, and it will certainly reach Bauman bin Qulesh for his wickedness. Bauman bin Qulesh has made unpardonable mistakes this time, because he has destroyed and tortured God's creatures. Hence, God also must destroy him. I am a pious man and I believe God's word which he revealed in his book – The Koran, which says: "Say to those who reject faith: 'Soon will you be vanquished and gathered together to Hell, - an evil bed indeed (to lie on)". (Imran: 12). Also God had revealed: "Of such the reward is that on them (rests) the course of God, of his angels, and of all mankind; - in that they will dwell; nor will their penalty be lightened, nor respite be their (lost)". (Imran: 8)-88). "Believe in God; for he is not stupid, my lady!".

The words of Hakiym Hashim and his advice encouraged Rasheed's mother greatly, and she had faith in her lord, as he alone can cause life and death, and there is no creature that can compete with God.

Bauman bin Qulesh used to live in the mountains. He built his house there and lived alone with his daughter. He had a very disgusting shape, and if one is not brave and fearless, he cannot stare at him. He was tall and very lean with extraordinary long neck and nose. His eyelids were thick and were not separated between his two eyes. He always used to paint his eyes with antimony. He had no hair except a little on the center of his head. He had long fingers and he used to keep long fingernails. He had a habit of keeping his tongue out and licking his lips as dogs do. He built his house adjacent to the rock and if one enters inside, he can also enter the rock. There was a large room inside the rock, which looked like a cave, and it had no built walls but the walls were part of the rock itself. It was very dark inside that room. The only light was from the fire lit on the poles fixed on the walls. The ground was sand, and there was an opening through which water enters and made a pool inside the room. The strangest thing was that even if the water entered for days or years, the size of the pool remained intact.

The question is, where did the water go as it never filled the room and never raised above the level of the pool knowing that the water poured in continuously! Besides the pool grew two trees of the height of a human being. On the branches of those trees were creatures of different kinds, such as owls, lizards and big wild birds. Also there were not less than twenty chameleons of different colours, small and big. At the center of the room was a big table made of pieces of the rock and on top of the table was an iron cage and inside it was a small bird which used to sing but it was invisible. If one looked inside the cage, it looked empty. Also there was a very big bowl made from the thick marble, and inside it was something, which looked like white water. It was not known whether it was real waters or something else, but it was boiling inside the bowl. It was something as if it was put on the fire and the smoke or vapour comes out from that water.

Bauman bin Qulesh was in his room at that time – the room in which he practices his wickedness. He used to enter that room daily and he took his piece of wood through which he angured everything he wanted to know. When he was inside the room, his daughter, Kamraash, entered and went to where her father was sitting. Bauman bin Qulesh was auguring in his piece of wood. He was quietly busy writing and canceling. Suddenly he stood up and changed in to a furious person and he told his daughter: "Rasheed is not seen in my piece of wood". Why? There must be someone who is interfering in my work! Is there anyone who has such ability? It is essential to investigate about Rasheed. Tonight, Oh Kamraash, we shall go to Rasheed to see for ourselves what is the matter with him. I have to destroy whoever attempts to arouse my anger-me! Bauman bin Qulesh!! When Kamraash heard that Rasheed is not visible in the augurs piece of wood of her father, said: "Before we go to Rasheed, it is better for you to send an envoy first who can investigate the situation and how things are over there. Send someone now, and if the envoy brings bad news, we shall ourselves go there to see". Bauman bin Qulesh accepted the ideas of his daughter, and went to the tree where the creatures were kept and picked up a snake and brought it to his table on which he practiced his sorcery. He kept the snake on the table and took special powder, which was in a small bowl and gave it to the snake. The snake licked all the powder, and then he took the snake and put it in the big bowl, which contained boiling water. Thereafter he talked to the snake, saying: "Raise up your head and listen to my instructions, Oh, my envoy!" After hearing the instruction, the snake, which was floating in the bowl, remained quiet and raised its head up. Bauman bin Qulesh told the snake: "Descent from all the mountains, cross all the rivers and avoid all creatures let they harm you, and go until you reach the house of Rasheed and get inside. Bring me news about Rasheed - I want to know his condition. If he has regained his life, then you know what to do; and if there is somebody else, who is interfering in my work, then kill him. Oh snake! Your poison is very strong; you should realise that if you fail to serve me you shall die by your own poison.

THE SORCERER AND
THE HEALER

Hakiym Hashim was sitting on the mat in the sitting room. He was touching his moustaches and looking outside through the window. Suddenly he felt that his moustaches were stiff and hard, and he called Bul Bul who was inside the room. When Bul Bul went to him, he asked him: "Tell me Bul Bul! What does your mind see at this moment?" Bul Bul sat down in front of Hakiym Hashim and held his head, which he directed downwards. He was contemplating or rather consulting his consciousness. He then raised his head up and replied to Hakiym Hashim: "Bauman bin Qulesh is busy at work. I feel that there is an envoy coming towards here from him". And Hakiym Hashim added: "Not only an envoy but it is coming to fulfil a bad errand. Poor Bauman bin Qulesh! He does not know that this world does not belong to him and he has no power to control it. The method, which he applies, is unlawful to be adopted by anyone who fears God, and that adopted by the God. Fearing person is blocked to him even if he attempts to follow it. Let his envoy come, as he will now realise that there are others who can challenge him".

The snake which was delegated by its master Bauman bin Qulesh came by descending the mountains and rocks where it lived, and crossed the rivers and the forests till it arrived to the fields of the farmers who were the friends of Bul Bul. It passed through all those tracks safely without being seen and headed to the house of Rasheed's mother.

Hakiym Hashim told Bul Bul: "When the envoy arrives, listen to the crying of the camels. They will begin braying before the arrival of the envoy, but when they stop, you should know that the envoy has arrived here. Bul Bul – you should go out to meet the envoy, and you should remember to do exactly as I tell you to do".

The snake heard the braying of the camels and went near the well, which was outside Rasheed's house. When it reached there the camels stopped braying and remained quiet looking at the wicked enemy who came to destroy. The door of the house was opened and there came out Bul Bul with the pot to take water from the well where the snake was hiding besides it. When the snake saw Bul Bul coming out it mistook him to Rasheed and in a hurry it rolled itself and kept ready waiting for a chance to bite. Bul Bul went near the well and stopped only a few steps from the well. He kept the pot down and retreated backward two steps. He said: "The envoy of Bauman bin Qulesh, you who have been delegated to do mischief – what you have been instructed to do is more difficult than your ability to fulfil. You cannot cross this sea for which you have come. You had better return to your master Bauman bin Qulesh and assure him that I, Rasheed am alive and have regained my life by the will of God. Go and tell him that the force of his witchcraft is deteriorating and that he shall soon perish. Tell him that God has cursed him together with all his associates, and that curse is certain, and if he does not believe, then I am waiting for his visit together with his daughter which they intend to make this night. Your poison will harm you and you had better go back." Bul Bul then turned back and returned in to the house, but before he entered the house, the snake jumped up with intent of biting Bul

Bul under his head. Bul Bul and Hakiym Hashim however, knew beforehand that, that would happen, and were fully prepared for anything. The pot, which was already instructed, lifted up and directed its mouth towards the snake, and unknowingly, the snake entered therein and the pot flew up in the sky straightaway towards the house of Bauman bin Qulesh.

Bauman bin Qulesh heard the door of his operation room being knocked, but when he opened the door he saw nothing. He went outside the door to look who had knocked but could not see anybody. He returned inside furiously and banged the door with force.

When he went to his desk he saw the pot, and he did not know who kept it there. He hesitated for a while, and then went to his desk and touched the pot, but the pot dropped from his hand and flew into the space. He became very shocked to see unusual thing like that. He thought to himself: 'what! Is this God's miracle or is it the trickery of human beings like me?" The pot stopped from hovering in the space and dropped in the ground and broke up into pieces. He saw his snake rolling itself lazily because of the torment it had suffered. Bauman bin Qulesh, with great anxiety and yearning to know what had happened, went to his snake and took it to his desk and dropped it into bowl of boiling water and said: "You snake, say what did you see where I delegated you. Give me a quick answer before you increase my fury and make me lose your life. Tell me how it came that you entered into the pot which flew you here?" After being put in a bowl with boiling water he put up its head and began to say: "Oh my master! I beseech you to soften your anger on me, I beg you to spare my life, because although the poison, which is in my mouth, does not harm me, it is nevertheless very strong and it will cause my death the moment it enters my body. The job which you instructed me to do is very difficult, my master! I failed to fulfil what you wanted me to do although I tried hard. Things were not as you expected. I saw Rasheed quite alright going and coming as he liked; and he gave me the following message to deliver to you: He says that the force of your witchcraft is deteriorating and you shall soon perish. He also said that God has cursed you and all your associates; your being cursed is certain and if you do not believe in what he says then he is waiting for your visit which you intend to make with your daughter tonight".

Bauman bin Qulesh became very furious and banged his desk with a fist saying: "Oh! You weak creature who does not feel sympathy with yourself and who does not like your soul; you have failed to serve me and to follow my instruction? You must perish!" Bauman bin Qulesh took the snake from the boiling water, and held its head with his right hand and its tail with his left hand. He turned its head till the middle of its body and pressed hard till the snake opened its mouth; and he put its body in its own mouth and pressed its mouth until its teeth penetrated into its own body. He then threw it down and buried it under the sand with his feet. Bauman bin Qulesh then shouted and called his daughter Kamraash. When Kamaraash heard the voice of her father calling with anger, hurried up and went to her father to hear what had happened. When she went to her father, she found him in a state of rage, which changed his appearance and his character. She never remembers to have seen her father in such a state of rage and anger before, and she said: "My father, you have called me and I have come". Bauman bin Qulesh said angrily: "Failure of that creature which I delegated to serve me were your ideas. You wanted to weaken me so that I appear low. Rasheed!!! Your Rasheed has the ability to tell me that I am cursed and my witchcraft has now perished, and that soon I shall myself perish by the will of God – as if he knows the secret of God. Even that Rasheed is trying to show me his teeth – I, Bauman bin Qulesh who, merely by hearing my name, everybody in this kingdom trembles! If he wants to lose his life, then he shall lose it. But the origin of all this, is you Kamraash! Because your heart which never relates to love a man every now and then, and everyone you love, in the end does not respond and runs away from you, and then you want me to destroy him. Today is the day, and Rasheed must be totally destroyed. Get ready to go to war because the message, which he sent to me, says that if I do not believe in his message that I shall perish, then he is waiting for my visit, which I intend to make this night together with you. You should know that immediately after sunset we shall go to face Rasheed; and he should show me his strength which he possesses".

Kamaraash began to think and to put into consideration the words she had heard from her father. She then asked her father: "Father! Tell me, how Rasheed could know that the snake was an envoy which you had send to harm him?" And how could he know that we intended to go to him tonight? I believe without any doubt, that Rasheed is not the same Rasheed who used to come here with his stupidity of love. This is a Rasheed who must have changed completely. The question is, where has he acquired all this force even to an extend of challenging with rudeness? My Father; please accept what I am telling you. My mind hesitates about Rasheed. It may be true that he has the ability to do anything against you and without being afraid of you. It is better for us to be careful". Bauman bin Qulesh said: "Let me see him if truly he is not afraid of me, and the truth and falsehood of your doubts will be exposed tonight when we shall go there".

THE DESTRUCTION OF
THE GREAT SORCERER AND
HIS DAUGHTER

After saying his night prayers (Isha), Hakiym Hashim told Bul Bul: "Today is today Bul Bul, either they or we". Fighting will begin in a short while. Bauman bin Qulesh and his daughter Kamraash will come, in what shape we do not know, but may be will come disguised as animals so that they should not be recognised. We must make Rasheed's mother unconscious because she will not tolerate the frightening scene which will happen here. She may even upset all arrangements which we have kept ready to protect ourselves from the wickedness of Bauman bin Qulesh and his daughter Kamraash who seek to ruin us. I shall make her unconscious, and you, my son Bul Bul, today is your day of destroying the wickedness of Bauman bin Qulesh and his daughter completely. I see that he is beyond my position even to look at his face. Bauman bin Qulesh cannot do anything to harm you, and this is a fact I assure you. But you have to be firm because he will come with such frightening things that you have never heard or seen before. Today you shall see such things, and you need to have a bold heart and determination because it will not be easy not to relax and to be frightened. All the threats which Bauman bin Qulesh are his devices which he uses to check your ability and if you have any power to face him. You should not be afraid at all even if the earth will tremble and the heaven become furious. All that is false and a trifle which have no truth in them. Maintain your faith in God, because God himself knows that you, his creature, are today combating the wicked people who seek to destroy you. No doubt God will protect you. And we the elders together with God's angels will pray for you from the Almighty God. I have kept everything ready for you, and you should do as I told you to do without any hesitation. You should remember that they are two and you are alone, although I shall be ready to help you in case of any difficulty, but you should not be afraid because Kamaraash, the daughter of Bauman has no much strength and should not cause you troubles. She should be the first to be destroyed, and although the rage of her father will be very much increased when he shall see his daughter destroyed, but they deserve to be annihilated for their wickedness and their ruthlessness against the lives of their fellow human beings. You should remember one very important thing my son, that Bauman bin Qulesh is only a sorcerer, and that is his own wickedness which do not come from God. Before you enter in to fighting with him, you should recite the verse of *Kursy (from holly Qur'aan)* loudly and you should translate it so that he should hear what you say. When he knows that you are a pious person, and you depend upon God, he will be filled with hesitation".

After giving Bul Bul all the details, Hakiym Hashim went to Rasheed's mother and told her that it would be better for her to go to bed early that night. He made her unconscious and kept her on her bed. He then went to where Bul Bul was sitting and told him: "Keep your ears awake, and when you hear the braying of the camels in the hut you should know that your enemies have arrived. I have already told you what you should do. I pray to God to protect you from all the wickedness of Bauman bin Qulesh and all his wicked associates".

Bauman bin Qulesh and his daughter Kamraash arrived and came near the lawn of Rasheed's house, but did not come in the shape of human beings. They disguised themselves as two big wild dogs that live in the forest. They came as two very big wolves.

The camels began to move around the hut after smelling the smell of the wicked persons. God has gifted all animals with ability to sense quickly the presence of both the wicked and the good. After waiting for some time, the two dogs went to the house, and when they reached the well, the door of the house opened and Bul Bul came out. He walked about two steps and stopped.

Bauman bin Qulesh and his daughter in wolves shapes after seeing Bul Bul whom they thought was Rasheed, the two dogs began to be furious and began to roar like lions exposing their teeth, lifting their mouths up and stared with sharp eyes like mad dogs. Since it was the night of moonlight, Bul Bul could see all the unusual things, which the dogs did. The dogs roared more and more and scratched the ground causing much dust to fly up. Bul Bul remained quiet with his hands tied up just looking. When they saw that Bul Bul was not frightened with their activities, the two dogs stood on their hind legs and directing their mouths upwards they cried aloud as they did before. Bul Bul then began to tell the dogs: "you Bauman bin Qulesh, stop your noise, that will not frighten me. Open your ears and listen to God's word." Bul Bul then recited the verse of *Kursy* and then translated it: "God! There is no God but he, the living, the self-subsisting, eternal, no slumber can seize him nor sleep. His are all things in the heavens and on earth. Who is there can intercede in his presence except as he permitteth? He knoweth what (appeareth to his creatures as) before or after or behind them. Nor shall they compass aught of his knowledge except as he willeth. His throne doth extend over the heavens and the earth, and he feeleth no fatigue in guarding and preserving them for he is the most high, the supreme (in glory)". (Baqra: 255). These are God's words whom I believe, so, if you have come with a belief that you have the ability to do what you wish – you Bauman bin Qulesh; then I, Rasheed challenge you. If you have that ability, then show me something more than what you had done before such as changing my body into a stone. My body has now regained its original form, and as you now see me in front of you – a complete human being. This is a good evidence to show you that your power is no more, and you are nothing but a hypocrite and a liar. It is God's curse which afflicts you now. The stone has regained its original form, and your envoy could not serve you and it returned back to you. You have seen all these events with your own eyes and you now know that you are not worthy of anything anymore. You have to think very well whether you will be able to fulfil your desire, which has brought you here. Or do you want to exhibit your power which you no longer possess? So, go ahead Bauman bin Qulesh, I am here ready to deal with you. But you should remember that any wickedness which you shall attempt to make implement this night will cause the loss of your daughter's life Kamraash in front of your eyes".

Bulbul aim his arrow to the big falcon who came to attack

When Bauman heard the statement of Bul Bul, he told his daughter Kamraash (in an animal language without uttering a word) to go and bite Bul Bul's throat until he dies. The dog promptly ran towards Bul Bul, Bul Bul kneeled down and picked up a handful of sand and kept himself fully prepared to meet Kamraash. The dog jumped up seeking to bite Bul Bul on his throat but Bul Bul was very quick to throw the sand on her eyes and she fell down crying loudly because of the pain in her eyes. Bul Bul held the tail of the dog and lifted it up. He then flew it up and it banged down in the hut of animals. The animals that were looking at all the events unanimously attacked the dog when it fell in their hut. The goats used their horns; the camels used their legs and the sheep their heads. They attacked it and crushed it completely until it was not possible to recognize its face and head. Here Bul Bul told Bauman bin Qulesh: "You have seen with your eyes the death of your daughter because of your wickedness. Other God's creatures have managed to kill your daughter Kamaraash, because although they are animals, they understand who is wicked and a tyrant. They know that she was the cause of my turning into a stone. Now it is your turn Bauman bin Qulesh! Here is a battle field and here I am a fighter come into the battle field and fight if you have the power". Bauman bin Qulesh with increased fury for the death of his daughter, changed himself in to big bird and flew into the air, and then came down towards where Bul Bul was standing with great speed, and when he reached him, he lifted him with one of his legs and flew with him in the air. He went so far high until he was seen very small. At that time Hakiym Hashim seeing that Bul Bul had been taken came out quickly and put off his turban and spread it on the ground; and after reciting his prayers he closed his eyes and directed his head towards the heavens in order to pray to God. He then stretched his hand on the turban, which he had spread on the ground. The turban lifted itself up like a strong mat, and flew up into the air.

Bauman, or the big bird, after reaching very high in the air, dropped Bul Bul so that he should fall down and die. Bul Bul felt that he was going to die because he could not think what could save him from death. The turban on the other hand flew up in the air till it reached the space where Bul Bul was dropped. It was fully spread like a mat. Bul Bul, trusting in God, recited his prayers silently, then he saw the turban flew towards him and dropped on it. He found himself sitting on a long piece of cloth which was flying towards the ground. Such miracles surprised Bauman very much and he realised that it was very difficult to defeat this young man. "Has he escaped this fate?" But he was not yet satisfied, and he thought he would deal with him when he came down. The turban descended softly until it touched the ground, and Hakiym Hashim held Bul Bul in his hand and disembarked him. He then took his turban and wrapped it on his head. He told Bul Bul: "your enemy is coming back, and it is high time now to destroy him. Wait! I shall go inside and will return in a moment." Hakiym Hashim went inside the house and came out with a bow and three arrows which he gave to Bul Bul. He told him: "Strike him on his chest with an arrow before he touches the ground. Be very careful not to miss him. If you miss him, he will attack you and destroy you because that is his intention now. If your arrow hits him on the chest, you should know that you have finished him, but you should be ready to attack him again until you plant all the three arrows in his body".

The big bird was coming down with great speed towards Bul Bul and it was carrying a very big rock with its feet. When it saw Bul Bul it aimed the rock at him and then dropped it so that it could destroy him. Bul Bul saw the rock dropping though it was far from him. He knew it was aimed at him. He raised his hand and directed it towards the rock and prayed. The rock stopped and remained motionless in the air. He instructed it to descend slowly to the ground, and the rock obeyed the instructions and dropped on the ground slowly. The bird realised that the young man was not as he thought him to be. His knowledge is great and essentially God is assisting him, as there is no sorcerer who remembers God in his sorcery. The bird still up in the air nery close to Bul bul, carefully Bul Bul threw his arrow towards the bird. It pinched the right place, and penetrated into the chest. The bird yelled loudly and screamed very much and its voice frightened people who were far away.

Rasheed's mother was awakened by the frightening cry. She got up from her heavy sleep and went out to see what was happening. She saw that a big bird which she had never seen before – bigger than their house- was baffling with pain and blood was gushing forth from its chest. Bul Bul hurriedly fixed another arrow to his bow and aimed it at the bird, but the bird quickly changed itself into its original form of a human being – Bauman bin Qulesh – while the arrow was still planted in his chest. He kneeled down with one of his hands holding the arrow and with another hand beseeching Bul Bul not to throw another arrow at him. He was saying: "Please spare my life Rasheed! Your arrow has destroyed me and consumed my strength because it is very painful". Bul Bul replied to him saying: "You Bauman bin Qulesh, you are wrong! I am not the Rasheed you think of, My name is Bul Bul, the student of the great healer who is famous throughout the world who does not follow the way you do by harming people. On the contrary, he helps them and heals their diseases and much more. Your wickedness, which you have been practicing throughout your lifetime, is what caused us to come here after many days of hardship and problems which we endured to seek you. You have destroyed the lives of parents who had to look after their children, the lives of children who were like gifts in the hearts of their parents and lives of husbands who were beloved to their wives. You have done all that without regard to such sweet life of those who adore each other. You considered yourself possessing all abilities, never thinking that there were people who could challenge you in this world. Belief in God escaped your heart and you considered yourself the giant who could not be challenged by anyone. Where is your power now Bauman bin Qulesh? Where is your capability which you came to show me today? Who among two of us is being destroyed at this moment? You are now finished Bauman bin Qulesh and there is nothing remaining with you. Your life is no more, and you very well know what God has kept in store for you. You are going straight to the Hell of fire like those who had disobeyed their Lord from the beginning to the end of the world".

"Bauman bin Qulesh, if you do not know that I am the student of who, then listen and see with your own eyes a person who is endowed with great knowledge and much experience and ability to detect the wickedness of the people like you. Open your eyes now and look at him while you still retain your wickedness".

Hakiym Hashim came forward in front of Bauman bin Qulesh who was set with blood and the arrow still in his chest. He told Bauman: "I never thought that you were weak like this, but you have no ability at all. You used to deceive yourself with the activities of hypocrisy and sorcery. How many have you tortured and humiliated with your sorcery? How many have you created and gave life as the true God does? How many more do you think you can oppress and challenge? Just look at your condition now, Oh Bauman bin Qulesh! Perhaps you forgot that you were also created and was given life by he who has that ability. Before you lose your life, there is something which you must do. Inside this house, there is the body of the young man – Rasheed – which until this moment is still in the form of a stone. This young man whom you see here is not Rasheed. He is Bul Bul, my student, who with the will of God, he caused them to look similar. They resemble one another without any difference. Perhaps it was God's will that Bul Bul should come here to help Rasheed and to expose you Bauman bin Qulesh who were notorious and who used to frighten the people of this country, with your wickedness. There is a man in the country where we come from – in the islands Zanzibar in East Africa lying in the Indian Ocean – there is a man known as Sheikh Nahwandy and his real name is Mohammed Farha. With your wickedness, you have also turned him into a stone similar to Rasheed. Bauman! You have to change them into their normal shapes of human beings so that they can return to their natural lives as granted to them by God. You should remember that the reason of your turning them in to stones is the envy of your daughter. Where is your daughter now? She has already lost her life as she caused the lose of the lives of many people. Return the normal conditions of both Rasheed and Sheikh Nahwandy, and we shall have no cause to quarrel with you anymore".

The screaming of Bauman bin Qulesh resulting from the pain of Bul Bul's arrow when he was still in the form of the bird, reached the village of the farmers – the friends of Bul Bul. They were anxious to know what had happened. Thus they went collectively to find out what thing or what animal had such a frightening screaming. They followed the yelling until they reached Rasheed's house. They saw and heard every thing said by Bul Bul and Hakiym Hashim to Bauman bin Qulesh whom they saw in a condition prior to his death while the arrow was still in his chest. Some of them saw Bauman bin Qulesh for the first time.

THE GREAT SORCERER REPENTS

B auman bin Qulesh understood that his life was no more and he would die very soon, so he said: Oh, you Mister who is very wise together with this clever young man Bul Bul, I consent that even if a person is a sorcerer like myself; there is much in life which he misses. Never believe that there is anyone who possesses or may possess everything called life. I was in the world of darkness. I never felt any sympathy and did not know faith in my heart regarding consideration for my fellow human beings as this clever lad had just told me. The words, which you have told me today, are facts though I come to realize at the zero hour of my life. I have disobeyed my lord very much without caring that he is there and that he will punish me. I do not think that because of many sins I have committed during my life, God will pardon me. I nevertheless repent to him and ask for his forgiveness and I accept any punishment which he may choose to punish me. Hakiym Hashim! Rasheed and Sheikh Nahwandy will essentially regain their noconditions, but, at this zero hour of my life, I beseech you to give me advises with your tongue which is gifted with the language of wise words. Tell me, if even me, a person who has much sins, may be pardoned by God".

Hakiym Hashim told Bauman bin Qulesh: "God's patience is greater than the whole world. God has mercy to his servants. That was not in your heart after disobeying your Lord for many aggressions against your fellow creatures. But it is not strange now to hear you speak these words. It is tantamount to The Pharaoh during the time of Moses. He tortured his people and made himself God to his people. His wickedness made God to annihilate him after rejecting God's command sent to him through Moses. When he was drowning in the sea he pleaded guilty and declared he was not God and that Allah is the true God. That however, did not save him and he was destroyed". "Bauman bin Qulesh! There is nobody who knows the secret of God. I cannot say yes or no that God will pardon you or will punish you. You had better pray to him to forgive you because he is most forgiving and most merciful".

After listening to the advice of Hakiym Hashim, Bauman bin Qulesh said: "After my death, both Rasheed and Sheikh Nahwandy will regain their normal conditions, but I shall not be here to apologize and ask for their forgiveness". Hakiym Hashim just nodded his head, and immediately Bauman bin Qulesh perished. The gathering of the people who were there to witness the death of Bauman bin Qulesh were greatly surprised to see that young man, Bul Bul had managed to finish Bauman bin Qulesh with his cleverness; Bauman who was being feared by everybody.

Rasheed's mother who came out to see Bauman bin Qulesh from the time he re-changed himself to his human shape until his death remained tongue-tied just looking at Bul Bul and Hakiym Hashim. She had never seen a person who had a brave heart like Bul Bul. She went to where he was standing and both the bow and an arrow still in his hands. She looked at Bul Bul and touched his cheeks while smiling as if she wanted to cry. Tears were flowing from her eyes. She held Bul Bul's head and kissed him on his forehead, right cheek and left cheek. Then she said: "Bul Bul! Today is one of the days of my life during which I have enjoyed the world. I have seen with my own eyes the miracles of God. If what I have seen was just a mere tale, it would have stimulated my body and I would have wished to see. But having seen this historical event which can never be forgotten by all the people who are present here. She turned to the farmers who were her neighbours who had come there to witness the destruction of Bauman bin Qulesh the famous notorious sorcerer of Morocco, and told them: Oh you my brethren! You have seen with your own eyes all that had taken place here. This event must be known by all the people throughout the world. Where are the writers of history? If amongst you there is anyone who likes to write about history, then this event must be recorded so that it should not be forgotten in the world, both present and in the future. The names of Hakiym Hashim and Bul Bul must be written in golden ink in such history books. It should be a lesson to many who would wish to oppress others who are weak and who cannot defend themselves. It should be a lesson to such wicked people who seek to torture, injure and do injustice to the weak by depriving them of their happiness. There is no being who is perfect and possesses everything except God done. These words were spoken by Bul Bul just now when he was addressing Bauman bin Qulesh whom all of you- people of this country – were afraid of him more than he who deserves to be feared. For many years he kept you in such a situation, and you lost hope that there could be anyone who could challenge him and put to an end the wickedness and aggression of Bauman bin Qulesh. Where is he now! Only his name remains!"

All the people there celebrated the success of Bul Bul and Hakiym Hashim for their bravery to be able to finish Bauman bin Qulesh -— the mischievious sorcerer – and his wickedness.

RASHEED REGAINS HIS HUMAN SHAPE

B auman bin Qulesh said in his last hour of life that both Rasheed and Sheikh Nahwandy – Namira's father – would regain their human shapes immediately after his death. Thus, when Bauman bin Qulesh died, Rasheed changed from a stone to his human shape. He woke up, and in a state of not knowing what had happened to him, he thought that he just had a long and deep sleep for many hours. Because of the shouting outside the house where people were celebrating the death of Bauman bin Qulesh, Rasheed attempted to sit down to listen to such shouting or about which he did not know anything. Before he left the bed, he felt that something was tied on his right hand, and when he looked at it, he found that it was a charm. He also felt his body heavy and fatigued to the result that he was helpless. Nevertheless he dragged himself and crawled to the door. When he raised up his eyes he saw his mother standing at the center of the crowd and surrounded by the village farmers. She was making a short speech. He remained at the doorway and listened.

When his mother finished her speech, the farmers saw Rasheed and immediately all the eyes turned towards the door in a great surprise. Everybody was looking at Rasheed and Bul Bul alternately as if to wish to know how these two persons resembled one another as if they were twins.

When Rasheed's mother saw her son standing at the doorway, she ran to him quickly and hugged him hard and began to kiss him madly. Tears were running from her eyes. She began to speak in a stumbling voice questioning her son: "Rasheed, my son, how are you – Are you alright?"

After greeting him in that manner, she explained to him everything that happened in the house and the role which the famous healer Hakiym Hashim and his student played in healing him. He commended Bul Bul as a brave young man and how he destroyed the wicked sorcerer Bauman bin Qulesh and his daughter Kamraash. She then bade farewell to her neighbours the village farmers who dispersed and returned to their homes. Then Rasheed's mother requested Hakiym Hashim and Bul Bul to get inside the house; he was looking at Bul Bul in a surprise as if he was wondering how he resembled him so much. When they got inside the house he took him to the lamp which was fixed to the wall and looked again at his face. He then caressed him. "This is God's will and his grace" he exclaimed! After Rasheed was satisfied with his curiosity, his mother went to Bul Bul and told him: "Bul Bul, my son! You have already seen how Rasheed was looking at you. No wonder he likes you very much, and since he has no brother, he wishes to request you for something but his tongue is hesitating. So I request you on his behalf to stay with us here without going anywhere. We will do everything for you". Bul Bul smiled and then said: "Surely, mother, I would be most pleased to live with you here, particularly as I would have the company of a brother like Rasheed; but I cannot – in fact I do not have the courage to decide because back home, in the islands of Zanzibar, I left my mother whose only son is me, as I have already explained to you before. So I have no choice but to return home to

Zanzibar and to ask for my mothers opinion. I promise you that if she agrees, I shall come back here to live with my brother".

Bul Bul's statement drew tears from Rasheed's mother. She stood up and began to kiss Bul Bul on both cheeks. Rasheed, on his part, also hugged Bul Bul and kissed him with much affection, and beseeched him no to leave them.

Dhow "Mabruka" entering the island of Zanzibar

BUL BUL
AND HIS TEACHER
GO HOME

Hakiym Hashim and Bul Bul remained as guests of Rasheed and his mother for seven days, and thereafter Hakiym Hashim told Rasheed's mother that they had to leave. He bade her farewell and told her that it is time to return to their homeland – the islands of Zanzibar in East Africa. He told her that they had to complete their work, which actually brought them to the country of Morocco. Being convinwith their reasons, Rasheed's mother had no choice but to bid them farewell but tears of happiness dropped from her eyes as an expression of her thanks. So they left.

Their journey to Djibouti took them twenty days. When they reached there, they went to the port and asked about the same Dhow which brought them there from Zanzibar – the Dhow named 'Mansura'. Unfortunately they were told that the Dhow had already left for its home port of Oman. So they had to travel on another Dhow named "Mabruka". When they reached to the Island of Zanzibar, they found Bul Bul's mother was sick. Namira, however, was taking care of Bul Bul's mother for all her needs. Namira, Sheikh Nahwandy's daughter, however, could not do much about Bul Bul's mothers sickness which was God's will as well as her great yearning to see her son Bul Bul who had left for quite a long time. But with the will of God, when she saw her son again she became well, and on that day she ate well more than usual and became happy.

BUL BUL WEDS NAMIRA

On the next day Bul Bul and Hakiym Hashim went to Namira's house. When they reached there, they were received with much rejoice. It was quite a warm welcome. Namira, her mother and her sisters embraced Bul Bul and Hakiym Hashim as a token of their thanks and an expression of their merriment.

Bul Bul and Hakiym Hashim understood that their work was completed; that Sheikh Nahwandy had already regained his human form. Namira began to explain to Bul Bul and Hakiym Hashim everything and said: "Truly, it was like a miracle before our eyes. I thus thanked God for enabling you to heal my father and to bring back to him his human form. Every time when I say my prayers I pray to God to bring you back to Zanzibar peacefully and safely".

Hakiym Hashim then explained all the story about their journey and the events they had encountered. The story surprised everybody particularly the sea voyage to Djibouti and their combat with Bauman the great sorcerer – and his daughter Kamraash. Sheikh Nahwandy then returned to the house and when he entered inside, Namira in excitement, quickly introduce him to Hakiym Hashim and Bul Bul. She told her father that they were the cause of his regaining his human form.

With great pleasure Sheikh Nahwandy thanked Bul Bul and Hakiym Hashim, and faced Bul Bul and told him: "In fact I have no better way of expressing my thanks and no suitable gift or any payment which will satisfy my heart except to request you to marry my daughter Namira". He then asked his daughter: "What is your opinion Namira? And Namira promptly replied: Daddy! That thing was in my mind before you mentioned it; and if you had not mentioned it yourself, I myself would have mentioned it to you". Sheikh Nahwandy embraced his daughter and kissed her, and on the next day he brought the Religious Judge to read the marriage contract.

Much celebrations were held and many people from all the villages and the whole township area of Zanzibar town were invited and entertained. It was quite a historical event and the marriage of Bul Bul and Namira was the talk of the town.

THE END

Written by Jawad Ibrahim Ahmed Al Bahrani
Translated from Swahili to English by
H.E. Ahmed Hamoud Al-Ma'amary